TO THE DEATH

Nantaje caught the flicker of indecision in the man's eyes an instant before his mouth tightened and his hand sprang for the revolver on his hip. The Apache lunged, the growl of a wild animal in his throat as they clashed and tumbled farther down the hill. The white man was big, with bulk and weight on his side, but Nantaje's sinewy muscles belied his size. Arms bulging like corded steel cables, his fingers clamped about the wrist of his gun hand while the white man struggled to hold Nantaje's knife at bay. They came to a stop with the scar-faced man on top. But wiry and quick, Nantaje twisted out from beneath him.

The gun roared near Nantaje's ear. . . .

The Outcasts series by Jason Elder:
#1: THE OUTCAST BRIGADE
#2: BLACK JUSTICE

OUTCASTS

WAR HATCHET

JASON ELDER

LEISURE BOOKS   NEW YORK CITY

A LEISURE BOOK®

November 2000

Published by

Dorchester Publishing Co., Inc.
276 Fifth Avenue
New York, NY 10001

ISBN 0-8439-4797-7

WAR HATCHET

Chapter One

Pots and pans clattering to beat the band, chickens squawking, bottles of *Hostetter's Celebrated Stomach Bitters*, *Dr. Kilmer's Female Remedy*, *Sherman's Pricklyash Bitters*, and a hundred other remedies, tonics and regulators rattling in their wooden crates, the heavy-sprung wagon bucked and swayed its way across the prairie, sounding like a collection of junk in a windstorm. Alroy Gallagher's Traveling Apothecary, Notions, and Dry Goods wagon was the only thing moving for miles around—except, maybe, for the antelope bounding for safety, or the prairie dogs scurrying to their holes, pausing only long enough to stare at this strange apparition that had invaded their world before plunging down them.

Up in the seat box Cubby Gallagher watched the ribbon of road unwinding ahead of them. Just two ruts slicing through a sea of tall grass, browning and brittle this late in the summer. All around him grassy hills rose and fell like great gentle waves rolling across the landscape. Far to the west he could just make out the purple haze of a distant mountain range, its name unknown to him. This was unfamiliar land. He recalled the brick buildings that stood tall along the straight streets, with their curbs and sidewalks. He pictured shop windows lit with gas lights. Poignant memories. Denver City seemed a long piece off now. When he thought of all he had left behind, a lump filled his throat and moisture stung at the corners of his eyes.

Cubby grabbed for the handhold as the clattering wagon thumped into a hole in the road and the team of horses shouldered against their harnesses to haul it out. The man on the seat beside him clucked impatiently and snapped a whip above the offside horse's ear. "Step lively now, Sal, we ain't got all day, you know!" Alroy Gallagher barked.

The wagon hurried on. Alroy was driving faster than usual, and looking over his shoulder a lot. Cubby clutched the iron handhold and clamped his hat to his head as a gust of wind cut across the road and pressed at the grass as it made its drunken way across the prairie.

"You've been mighty quiet," Alroy said, glancing over at him.

Cubby stretched out his legs, the tips of his shoes barely finding the toe board. Without proper anchorage he was having trouble staying in the seat. "I'm looking out for Indians, Uncle Alroy."

"Indians?" the man scoffed. "Not many redskins around these parts anymore. Army's done took care of 'em. But if some do show up I got Colonel Colt's new hammerless twelve bore right here to treat with 'em." Alroy gave the shotgun an affectionate pat.

Cubby's grip tightened around the iron armrest, his teeth clattering as another pothole intercepted a wheel. "Uncle Alroy?"

"What!"

Cubby recoiled some at the curt reply. "Why do I have to go and live with Aunt Doireann? Why can't I stay with you? I don't even know her. She and Ma—well, you know."

"Best not call her that when you are around her."

"But you—"

"What I call her out of earshot is one thing, Cubby. She used to go by that name, but ever since she up and married that railroad man Horace Taylor, she's had her nose all up in the air. She goes by Doreen these days. Mrs. Doreen Taylor. Even her being widowed didn't change that. You just call her Aunt Doreen and you two will get along fine."

Cubby frowned and thought life awfully unfair. It wasn't so unusual for a boy to lose his mother, or his father, but both, and at the same time. . . . He felt the sting return to his eyes and quickly brushed it away with the dusty sleeve of his shirt. Alroy's fist clamped lightly upon his shoulder. "It'll be all right," he said, more gently this time. Doireann will take good care of you. She'll see that you get your schooling, and that you have proper clothes to wear and food to eat."

Cubby sniffed. "But she doesn't know I'm even coming out to live with her. What if she don't want me?"

"She's blood relation, Cubby."

"So are you."

Alroy stiffened at that and removed his hand from the boy's shoulder and grabbed up the reins again. "The kind of life I live is no life for a youngster."

"You mean like what happened last night?"

"That's part of it," he said ruefully.

"Is that why you are driving so fast, why we left town in the dead of night?"

Alroy's face wrinkled as a frown worked its way across it. He needed a shave, but they had been in too much of a hurry to leave for him to lather his cheeks and scrape them clean. "Sometimes I got to deal with unpleasant people, Cubby. But more important, I go on from town to town, never staying long enough in one place to hardly read a local newspaper. How do you expect to get any schooling like that?"

"I already know reading and my numbers, Uncle Alroy."

"You hardly know enough to get by." Alroy shot a worried glance back along the side of his wagon. Cubby looked back too, over the top, past the cages tied there filled with squawking chickens flapping their wings, their clawed feet clutching the wooden bars to keep upright. He didn't see anything.

"Uncle Alroy?"

"What is it now?" he asked, raising his voice to be heard over the rumble of the iron-rimmed wheels.

"How come Ma never went to visit Aunt Doire— er, I mean Aunt Doreen?"

He looked at the boy. "Mean she never told you?"

Cubby shook his head.

"Well, I guess you were a mite young."

"I'm ten now."

Alroy grinned. "Yes, you are. Practically all grown up and ready to be on your own." Alroy paused, thinking it over, then said, "You know that your ma and Aunt Doireann grew up among the gentry, don't you?"

"What does that mean? I thought Ma grow'd up in New Orleans."

10

"She did, and her papa, your grandpapa, had himself a lot of money and fancy houses, and plenty of dark folks to work his farm—only they weren't called farms. They called them plantations." Alroy grinned. "I heard your grandpapa was quite a business man. Shrewd as they come. It's a pity you never had the chance to know him." Alroy's voice grew whimsical. "A pity I never knew him either. Maybe I wouldn't be piloting this peddler's wagon all over creation if I had. Your pa told me all about him."

"Did Ma and Aunt Doreen have a falling-out?"

"I reckon you're old enough to hear it now. Doireann was seeing a young man before the war; then he went off to West Point to learn how to become an officer. When the rebellion broke out her young man went right off to fight. He never did come back. Doireann waited, all the while watching the South, the only life she ever knew, burning to the ground around her. When Farragut finally wrestled control of the Mississippi River away from the South, Doireann and your ma knew the war had been lost, but blood still flowed for some years after that. They were both young and pretty, and had never known a lick of hardship. Suddenly they were on their own, homeless, their family dead."

"Sorta like me?" Cubby said.

"Sorta. When the war ended your ma went to live with relatives in Iowa. Your Aunt Doreen kept looking for her young man until she finally got word that he had died in a fierce battle. Having nowhere left to go, she joined your ma. The Union Pacific was working to build the transcontinental railroad right there across the river at Omaha, in Nebraska Territory. That was where Doireann met Horace Taylor. He was a young engineer with dreams of moving up in the company. And he did. He was right there

11

at Promontory Summit when they drove that golden spike. I seen the tintype Doireann has of that famous meeting of the two lines. Samuel Montague of the Central Pacific and Grenville Dodge of the Union Pacific are shaking hands among a crowd of men. Horace Taylor is about three faces to the left of Montague, tipping his hat to the camera, if I remember."

"But why did Ma and Aunt Doreen get mad at each other?"

"War changes people." Alroy frowned. "It changed Doireann. She didn't much like losing everything. And Horace Taylor, well, he had big ambitions. When two people like that get together they tend to lose sight of the important things. Money. Status. Suddenly that's all that's important to 'em. Your ma, she was about the sweetest gal I ever did lay eyes on. I many times wished it had been me instead of my brother she picked. She saw the change come over Doireann and tried to talk to her about it, but Doireann shut her out of her life. Shut her out completely.

Horace got himself a sweet job with the railroad as shipping agent for all of the U.P.'s western division. But that meant he had to live along the line, in Wyoming." Alroy paused, thinking it over. "Wyoming is not exactly the sort of place Doireann pictured herself ending up, but she moved there with Horace. Afterward the two sisters never had much to do with each other. There were a few letters, but not much more. Doireann and Horace built themselves the grandest house in town and always seemed to have more money than they needed." Alroy shook his head. "The railroad must have paid Horace right handsomely. Maybe I should have gotten into the railroad business myself."

Cubby thought it over, wondering if Aunt Doreen would take him in. Even though they were blood kin, she might not. After all, she and his ma had been blood kin too. "What if she won't have me?" he asked softly.

"Huh?"

He repeated it louder, above the rumble of the wheels.

"Don't worry about that. She asks about you whenever I come through. But if she won't, well, reckon I'll have to figure us out another plan, right?"

"Really? She asks about me?"

"Well . . . sure she does."

"What's she like?"

"She's a pretty woman. Tall, with black hair, though now it is showing some silver in it. Doireann is older than your ma was, but she don't look it."

"Why did she stay, Uncle Alroy?"

"You mean after Horace died?" Alroy snorted and shook his head. "I don't know. With all her money, you'd think she'd have taken herself back East. I don't know what keeps her in Jack's Fork. He looked briefly over his shoulder, then suddenly snapped his head around again. "Oh, no!" he groaned, giving the reins a sharp flick and reaching for the long-handled whip.

"What's wrong?"

"Trouble."

Cubby pulled himself up and peered past the chickens, past the plume of dust kicked up by the wheels. He saw them far off in the distance, just cresting one of the hills back there.

"Indians?" Cubby's heart leaped to his throat.

"I almost wish they was." Alroy snapped the whip. But even with the best of horses the heavy peddler's wagon could not outrun their pursuers.

The riders came on fast, four of them, and in another couple of minutes they caught up with the wagon, flanking it on both sides. Cubby recognized them, and suddenly he understood the reason for the terrified look that had come to his uncle's face.

"It's those men from town, Uncle Alroy. The ones causing all that trouble last night."

The riders closed in and turned the team off the side of the road. Alroy pulled the animals to a stop and sat there with his eyes going wider and his face looking a little like Cubby remembered his mother's face after baking bread. A tremble had come to his uncle's hand. One of the riders stopped in the road in front of the team and a tight smile touched his lips as two more rode up to Alroy's side of the wagon. The fourth drew rein near Cubby and glared at him. This one had a scar cut across his left eye and looked meaner than a basketful of scorpions. They were all dusty and sweating, and had that weary look about them that men sometimes get when they've been riding hard.

"I figured we'd catch up to you out here, you cheating snake-oil drummer!" one of the men said. Cubby remembered him from the other night. His name was Burl Rahn and he seemed to be the leader . . . at least he did most of the talking. He was a stubby man with a barrel chest, a stump of a neck and half a week's growth peppering his chin. He wore a wide hat pulled so low on his forehead that only his dark eyes could be seen scowling out from beneath the dusty brim.

Alroy gave a laugh that sounded a little like a bird twittering. He was sweating and his hands shook so hard, he had grasped his knees to keep them still. "Why, gentlemen, what ever are you talking about? I have cheated no man!" He tried to sound indignant, but the words came too quickly, too breathy for that. Cubby shriveled under their burning stares.

"You lying buzzard!" The man yanked a small bottle from a pocket inside his vest and waved it before Alroy's nose. "Remember this?"

Cubby remembered it all right. His uncle had given the bottle to these four right after they had declared Alroy to be a swindler before a crowd of people. "A peace offering," Uncle Alroy had professed, slipping Cubby a secret wink as he had handed it to the man. The label read *Dr. Esner's Double Action Depilating Cream.* He'd told the men it would thicken up the hair and make them irresistible to womenfolks. Cubby remembered Alroy's sly look afterward, and it was shortly after that that they'd quietly left town.

"Thicken my hair, will it? Make the women swoon at my feet, will it?" The man snarled, shoving the bottle so close to Alroy's face that his eyes crossed.

"It . . . it . . . it generally works on most men," Alroy squeaked.

The men all gave out a collective groan. "Then why didn't it work for us?" the spokesman roared and with that he whipped off his hat. A clump of brown fluff fluttered to the ground, and as the others tugged their hats off more drifted away like snowflakes on a winter's wind. "What do you think of this?" raged the man clutching out a fistful of hair and waving it at Alroy. "Look what you done to us!"

Some of them were showing more scalp than hair, and what little did remain looked like ragged islands floating on a sea of pink flesh.

Cubby would have giggled if he hadn't been so scared.

Alroy stammered. "I don't know what to say—"

The man near Cubby growled, "You done this on

15

purpose, mister, and we intend to make you pay for it."

"But I can assure yo—" Alroy's eyes expanded. "Wha . . . what are you doing?"

One of the men had nudged his horse near the wagon and lifted the latch on one of its doors. He grabbed out a collection of tin pans and tossed them into the road. They all proceeded to take target practice on them. When they had finished shooting up the pans, the man with the scar sliced the ropes and swept the chicken cages to the ground. They turned their guns on the squawking birds until blood and feathers splattered the road.

"Burn the wagon, Kleef," the leader ordered.

The one with the scar dragged Cubby from the box and dropped him to the ground.

"No, don't," Alroy pleaded. Pots and pans and bottles and bolts of cloth were scattered far and wide while gaily colored spools of thread and ribbons decorated the prairie grass, looking curiously festive but strangely out of place.

From where he had landed, Cubby watched the men gallop in a circle around his uncle's wagon, whooping like wild Indians, striking matches and setting fire to wads of paper that they tossed into the gaping doors, of which the wagon had plenty.

"Stop! Stop!" Alroy implored. He leaped to his feet and started off the wagon. A gun blasted and a bullet tore splinters from the wood at his feet.

Scarface—that was how Cubby thought of him— leveled his revolver. "You can just stay put, peddler! No man makes a fool of Lars Kersten and gets away with it!"

For Cubby, it was like the nightmares he used to have after his family's home had burned to the ground. Now, like those horrible dreams, it was happening all over again.

Alroy stood there as flames began licking out of half a dozen small doors on his wagon. "My horses. Let me cut my horses free," Alroy cried.

The animals were pawing the road. The head man had taken hold of Sal's bridle and was holding her in place. Cubby scrambled to his feet and grabbed the reins of Lars Kersten's horse, pulling hard. As its head came around, Kersten kicked out, catching Cubby alongside the head. "You'll be next if you don't mind your manners, brat!"

"Maybe we should let him off now, Burl," another man said.

"Not yet. I wanna see how long it takes to singe the hair off his head," Burl snarled.

Kersten was grinning, that scar twisting and folding along his cheek like a live worm. Panic swelled in Cubby's chest as the crackling flames leaped higher. He could smell the burning furs coming from inside the wagon and hear the popping of tonic bottles. Those bottles held nearly as much grain alcohol as they did medicinal fixings; he'd watched his uncle concoct most of it at night by their campfires.

Flames crawled up the side of the wagon, licking their way toward the seat box where Alroy was. Kleef said, "I think Cooper is right, Burl. Maybe we should let him off there." The fun had passed for a couple of them, but Kersten and Burl were enjoying Alroy's distress too much to end it right yet.

"I don't!" Burl snapped. "Let him burn a little."

Panic gripped Alroy. He was frying up there and it was about to get a lot hotter. The horses were wanting to bolt. Burl unchained them and they galloped off, stopping a few hundred yards out.

Cubby had to do something. . . . Picking himself

17

off the ground, he grabbed an iron skillet off the road and charged Burl, clunking him hard on the kneecap.

Burl howled in pain, his horse wheeling away from the attacking boy.

Atop the wagon, Alroy seized the opportunity and reached for the shotgun.

"He's got a gun!" shouted the one named Cooper.

Alroy pulled it out from under the seat and turned it on Burl. His finger groped through the trigger guard, but Lars Kersten was faster. The gunman's hand stabbed for the Colt in his holster, cleared leather in an eye blink and fired.

Alroy lurched back, his shotgun blasting. He clutched for the armrest, missed and fell from the high seat, hitting the ground hard.

Stunned, Cubby stopped beating on Burl and stood there, staring. Burl got his horse under control, leaped off it and backhanded the boy. Cubby's head spun and the next thing he knew he was lying in the grass, tasting blood. He hurt bad, and wanted to cry, but something rose up inside that stopped him. As his head cleared he could see the wagon in the midst of the inferno and feel the heat of it. A little way away two men were dragging Uncle Alroy away from the fire. They all stood around him then. Past the roar of burning wood and occasional pop of exploding bottles Cubby heard one of them say, "He's dead, Burl."

Kleef hunkered down over the body and felt for a pulse.

"He shouldn't never have reached for that gun," Kersten growled.

"Serves him right," Burl said, rubbing at his knee, looking pained. He ran his fingers through his hair and snarled at the clump that came off in his hand.

"Make a fool out of Burl Rahn, will you, peddler?" He spat at the body, then gave a short laugh.

Cubby sat up, too shocked to move. Cooper Brawley was shaking his head. "Now what are we going to do, Burl? He's *dead*, for Pete's sakes."

"Yeah," Kleef added. "That makes it murder."

"Nobody will know it was us," Burl said confidently.

"I don't know." Kleef frowned. "You made a lot of noise back in Dixon about how you was going to settle up with this drummer."

"Nobody will miss him," Burl said. "We'll throw the body in that burning wagon so there won't be no evidence against us. We'll go back to the ranch and act like nothing ever happened. Just won't go back to Dixon for a spell. We can do all our drinking in Jack's Fork, heh?"

"I reckon so," Kleef said, but there was uncertainty in his voice.

Cubby stood, confused, feeling the sudden weight of grief and a great despair. Uncle Alroy was dead, and he was alone . . . and then a new fear suddenly swept over him. And it was not a moment later that Lars Kersten turned his head and fixed his dark eyes upon him.

"We still got one problem, Burl," Kersten said.

"The kid!" Burl wheeled about to glare at Cubby.

Cubby's new fear had suddenly taken shape, clear as the ringing of a church bell.

"You aren't going to hurt the kid?" Cooper asked. They were all staring at Cubby now.

"He's the only one who can point a finger at us," Burl answered.

"Let me do it," Lars Kersten said. There was an unholy eagerness in his voice, a sneer giving life to that scar again.

Cubby didn't wait to hear any more. Half blind with fear he turned on his heels and shot for the hills. Behind him he heard a laugh, then Burl said, "Better go get him, Lars."

His uncle had wished they *had* been Indians. Now Cubby understood why. There was evil in these men . . . and now that evil was after him! Not daring to look back, Cubby strove on with all that his short legs could give. Arms pumping like pistons and the air burning his lungs, he raced across the prairie with the grass snagging at his shoes. There was a hill ahead and he aimed for it, hoping to find a safe haven on the other side. Fear clouded his eyes, but panic gave him a boost of speed that would have amazed him and his friends had it happened in another place and time.

He heard the pounding hooves growing louder behind him and chanced a look. Lars Kersten was coming on fast. The crest of the hill was just ahead, but in his heart Cubby knew that beyond it lay only more grass. There could be no help for him way out here, no place to hide, no end for his terror except the sort of end his Uncle Alroy had come to.

Lars was almost upon him.

Cubby burst over the crest of the hill. He plunged down the other side. Suddenly his eyes widened and his heavy breathing caught in his throat. Instinctively he feet dug in as he tried to stop himself, but his momentum carried him forward and he ran smack into the arms of his second greatest fear.

Indians!

Chapter Two

All morning Nantaje had followed the herd of an
telope, careful not to spook the wary beasts. Over
time they would get used to his presence—always
far off, yet always there. These animals had superb
vision, and even when their heads dipped to crop
the grass, their dark eyes were in constant motion.
But Nantaje was a patient man, and this was a game
he had played many times before. He had sometimes followed a herd of antelope all day. Eventually
they would get used to him being there, and when
they did he would work his way close enough for his
.45-70 Springfield rifle to do its job.

After a few hours the slim, tawny animals gathered in a bowl of brown grass and bedded down for
the afternoon. Their short black horns glinted in the
sunlight like claws of polished obsidian as Nantaje
worked his way to the brow of a hill and peered
down at them. He chose the buck among the harem

of does and eased the rifle to his shoulder. It was a far shot, even for the long-barreled military rifle. He considered the range, the weight of the bullet and its velocity and elevated the muzzle several feet above the resting animal. He caught his breath, and fired. At the sound of the rifle the startled herd leaped to their feet. The buck was just rising when it lurched around and dropped. Nantaje lowered the rifle and stood as the last of the fleeing animals disappeared over the next ridge.

He rode down to his kill. Over the months, Nantaje had taken over the duty of hunting for the group. They were six, an unlikely collection of men who had either chosen, or had been forced, to leave their own kind. Fate had brought them together, and a common goal kept them that way. California, named after a fabled city, held the jewels and pearls each of this group was after, but not the sort most would think of.

For John Russell Keane, the ex-army major, dreams of a peaceful Napa Valley vineyard called him west, but for Lionel, the black horse-wrangler, it was something else. He thought most often about the fine Spanish stallions waiting to be broken and sold.

Royden Louvel had only one thought, and that was to flee this country that had maimed him, conquered his beloved South and taken away his family estate in New Orleans. For Louvel, stepping off a pier in San Francisco and onto the deck of a schooner bound for Australia was his sole reason for riding with these men.

Dougal O'Brian felt much as Louvel did, only his hatred went further back, to the Mexican War. He had been one of the many Irishmen who had deserted Zachary Taylor's Army of Observation and swum the Rio Grande to join forces with Santa Anna's army. They had been called The San Patricio Battalion, renowned as some of the fiercest warriors in the Mexican Army. But in the end the warriors fell at the battle of Churubusco. O'Brian had been one of the eleven lucky ones. For his desertion he had only been branded on the cheek with a "D" and flogged. Sixty-five other San Patricios had been marched to the gallows by General Winfield Scott.

Afterward, O'Brian had fought for the Confederacy, becoming something of a demolition expert taking out railroad trestles that the North relied on. California seemed a safe haven to O'Brian, close enough to Mexico to scoot across the border whenever he got the urge. The señoritas there were reputed to be pretty and willing, and tequila plentiful. All the more incitements.

Harrison Ridere didn't hate the United States, only the army. He had walked away from Fort Huachuca one afternoon and never looked back. California was far enough away to give him breathing room, and like O'Brian, the Mexican border offered a bit of comfort, and the promise of pretty señoritas with eager arms.

And then there was Nantaje. The Indian gave a tight grin as he considered his own reasons. Apache by birth, Indian scout for General Crook by choice, Nantaje had burned his bridges at both ends. He was claimed by neither, now, and almost any place would have suited him just fine, so long as he could live there in peace. California just happened to offer the one thing this desert-born-and-bred man found intriguing. Water. Lots of water! He'd heard men talk of the Pacific Ocean, but could not imagine standing on land's end and seeing nothing but water stretching away to the horizon in all directions. This was his own personal jewel, and he was going after it.

California. A land not so many hundreds of miles to the west, yet for some reason a land as elusive as the end of a rainbow for these six men who always seemed to end up going the wrong way. They were traveling north this time. Not because they had any problems discerning the points of a compass needle, but because up north lay the tracks of the Union Pacific Railroad, and as John Keane had observed, "The railroad doesn't seem to have any trouble finding California, so why not just hitch a ride?"

The logic seemed sound enough, so north they pointed their horses with Nantaje always riding ahead. Hunting and scouting out a trail came as naturally to the Apache as roping and breaking a wild bronc did to Lionel. Or strategy and poker to Louvel. Keane, who sometimes forgot he was no longer a major in the army, had drifted naturally into the role of leader. The outcasts accepted that. Ridere, whose chief interest—other than pretty women, that is—lay in rapid-fire weapons of the sort that Mr. Gatling was building, was content to follow Keane. And so was O'Brian, so long as he could, from time to time, blow up something along the way. But O'Brian had left all his dynamite back at his cabin down in Mexico, and there hadn't been much of anything worth demolishing lately.

Nantaje quickly quartered the buck, taking the choice rump meat and leaving the rest for the coyotes and buzzards. He slung the haunches, hide still intact, over his horse and was about to leave when the sudden, distant pounding of hooves turned his head. He cocked an ear. There was something else too, something he couldn't immediately identify, but it sounded an awful lot like the ringing of a vast amount of iron. Was that bells, or was someone banging pots and pans? His curiosity piqued, he left the horse by the carcass and sprinted up the long grassy hill, dropping to his belly at its crest.

A few hundred yards off, the ruts of a road cut the prairie grass, and it was along those ruts that a peddler's wagon was hurdling itself, jostling side to side, swaying dangerously into a curve. The driver, a rotund fellow in a worn brown jacket, flailed the horses with his long buggy whip like a madman— then all at once Nantaje knew. The man wasn't mad, only frightened. Behind the wagon four riders had just come into view. They were gaining quickly on the wagon. There was a boy up on the seat with the driver, hanging on for dear life, and as the rattling and clanging grew louder, the Apache saw the terror that filled their faces.

The riders drew around the wagon and hauled it to a stop. There were words spoken—unfriendly words, but Nantaje was too far off to hear them. Whatever was said, the driver was shaking in his boots. Nantaje watched them ransack the wagon, spreading its wares across the prairie. They took to shooting up the stores and the chickens it had carried on its top. One of them yanked the boy from the seat and the rest galloped around the wagon setting fire to it.

Nantaje heard the man's plea, but they seemed intent on letting him burn with the wagon. The Apache scowled. This was none of his affair, yet the man and boy appeared helpless to save themselves from these men. Whatever had provoked the attackers, Nantaje knew there was injustice here, and he also knew that he must do something. He was outnumbered, but that was of no concern to him. Four whites against one Apache was the sort of odds his people had grown used to. It was about even, he judged. In fact, he figured he had the advantage since he carried a rifle, a revolver and his scalping knife.

Nantaje snapped open the Springfield's breech and slipped a round into the chamber. Resting the butt against his shoulder, he thumbed back the hammer. Down by the wagon the boy had suddenly grabbed a frying pan from the road and charged one of the riders, whaling into him. Seizing the opportunity, the driver up on the wagon reached for a gun, but the man was too slow. There was a shot and he toppled from the seat. The one getting the tar beat out of his leg leaped to the ground and slugged the boy.

It was too late to save the driver and Nantaje lowered the rifle to see what would happen next. They powwowed over the body a while, then turned their eyes toward the boy. Nantaje didn't like what he saw, and neither did the boy, for all at once he wheeled around and took off like a scared rabbit. As luck would have it, he had set a course straight for the hill where Nantaje lay in cover.

Nantaje judged the race between horse and boy. Boy had the lead but it was no contest. He saw the grin move across the rider's face and his thought instantly flashed back to another time and place. It was the same evil sneer he'd seen on the faces of the men who had once captured his people and murdered his brother-in-law. His mind suddenly made up, Nantaje shouldered the rifle again, but stopped just as his finger curled about the trigger. He reckoned the distance and knew the boy would make it over the hill—just barely. There was another way to do this. A way that would not attract the attention of the three men waiting down below.

He slipped back from the brow of the hill and dropped the rifle, drawing his scalping knife from its sheath. The pounding hooves drew nearer. Then the boy shot over the top of the hill. He spied Nantaje and tried to put on the brakes, and the next instant the Apache opened his arms and snatched the startled boy from his headlong flight. He swung him to one side and pushed him to the ground, spinning back around as the rider crested the hill. Nantaje sprang like a mountain lion, caught the man in his arms and dragged him from the saddle. They hit the ground together, momentarily stunned. Then the man shook the fog from his head and scrambled to his feet, rage replacing the surprise in his dark eyes. Nantaje was on his feet too, sunlight glinting along the blade of his knife.

A scar crawled sideways across the man's face as the man narrowed his eyes at the Apache. "What the hell?" he croaked.

"Are you so willing to fight a man as you are a boy?" Nantaje chided in English nearly as good as the other's. Years of living with the whites had taught him much. The language was only one of many things mastered during his years scouting for the white chief, Crook.

Nantaje caught the flicker of indecision in the man's eyes an instant before his mouth tightened and his hand sprang for the revolver on his hip. The Apache lunged, the growl of a wild animal in his throat as they clashed and tumbled farther down the hill. The white man was big, with bulk and weight on his side, but Nantaje's sinewy muscles belied his size. Arms bulging like cored steel cables, his fingers clamped about the wrist of the other's gun hand

27

while the white man struggled to hold Nantaje's knife at bay. They came to a stop with the scar-faced man on top. But wiry and quick, Nantaje twisted out from beneath him.

The gun roared near Nantaje's ear. The Apache drove a knee into his adversary's ribs, then twisted out of his grip and lunged. Eight inches of steel caught the man just below the ribs, and with a jerk, Nantaje drove the point of his knife up into his heart. He shuddered, his eyes huge and staring down unbelievingly. Then he collapsed.

Nantaje wrenched the knife free and suppressed the urge to give forth a howl of victory, knowing that that would attract the others by the burning wagon. Instead he sliced the scalp skin and pealed off the man's hair. There was something odd about the scalp. Clumps of hair came off in Nantaje's fist as he worked. But he had no time to ponder this. He had to move swiftly. Once their partner failed to return, they would come to investigate. He gathered the man's horse, slipped the rifle from its scabbard and thrust it barrel-first into the ground near the dead man. He placed the scalp upon the rifle's butt, snatched up the revolver and stuck it in his belt.

Turning, Nantaje found the boy riveted to the ground, staring in frozen fear.

"Come." Nantaje scooped him up and set him upon the dead man's horse. He hurried back to his own animal and swung up onto the saddle. Keeping the hill at his back to hide his retreat, and leading the dead man's horse, Nantaje slipped away unseen.

The sound of the revolver shot, muffled by the hill, brought a satisfied grin to Burl Rahn's face. The scowling lines softened and he said, "That takes care of our only witness."

Cooper Brawley cast a troubled glance at Kleef Langston.

Rahn laughed. "You two worry too much."

"I'm not worried," Langston said. "I just didn't see the need to kill the boy."

"You'd rather he put the finger on us?" Rahn shot back.

"No. Just wish we didn't have to do it, that's all."

"You're fretting like an old woman."

"Ah, lay off him," Brawley said. "I didn't want to see the kid killed either."

"You're both soft."

"We ain't soft about killing," Brawley went on, "we just don't take pleasure in it like some we know. Did you see the way Lars was grinning when he rode after the kid? He likes killing too much."

Rahn grabbed the dead man's arms and told Langston to take his legs. They heaved Alroy Gallagher onto the pile of burning timbers, then moved upwind of the stench of burning flesh. Rahn shifted his view to the hillside. "What's keeping Kersten?"

Langston frowned. "Knowing how he is around little boys, I don't care to think about it."

"The kid's dead," Rahn said.

Brawley shook his head. "The way Kersten gets sometimes, I wonder if that matters much to him."

Rahn slid a curious glance at Cooper Brawley. "How would you know about such things unless you like peeking?"

Langston laughed. "You two lay off each other. Maybe one of us oughta go and roust Kersten. We oughta be getting out of here. That wagon's putting out a lot of smoke. Likely to attract attention, and if it does, I don't want to be around when they come looking."

"Let's all go roust him out," Rahn said, starting for the horses. They mounted up and rode up over the hill.

Brawley was the first to see it. He tugged sharply at his reins and sat there staring as the other drew to a halt alongside him. No one spoke at first, then Langston let go with a low, heartfelt curse.

"Geeze, will you look at that?" Rahn gasped softly. He slowly dismounted, looking all around the rolling landscape. His shoulders had drawn tighter than a banjo string and his gun was suddenly in his hand. As he advanced he noted the half-butchered antelope below. He stood above Kersten's body, staring.

"Lars's been scalped," Rahn gulped, eyes widening at the sight of the mottled scrap of flesh draped over the rifle butt.

"Injuns!" Brawley declared grabbing for his gun and peering across the bowl at the ridge. "They're probably right over that rise."

Rahn studied the hilltops, then rushed back to his horse and grabbed up the reins. "Let's get the hell out of here," he said as he swung into his saddle.

"What about Kersten?"

"Kersten's past caring. Let him lay."

"And the kid?" Brawley asked.

"Injuns must have taken him." Rahn's eyes compressed as they swept around the grassy bowl one last time.

"That means there were witnesses," Brawley said worriedly.

"Maybe yes, maybe no. But I'll tell you one thing. I don't intend to stick around here and find out—not with scalping Injuns about. I'm cutting out right now." The sight of Kersten's scalpless corpse had shaken Rahn more than he would ever admit. "We'll worry about it latter." Reining his horse around, Rahn drove his spurs into its side.

The men rode away from there, swinging wide of the burning wagon and stench, and pointed their horses north, toward Jack's Fork.

Chapter Three

Nantaje left there swiftly but quietly, riding at a brisk gallop until the smoke of the burning wagon was but a distant smudge upon the horizon. When he'd finally gained enough distance to feel safe he stopped. The boy was rigid on the saddle, his round eyes staring, his face as unmoving as ice, and nearly the same color.

"It's all right," Nantaje said. "I don't think they will follow us—not with that warning I left behind."

The boy's view remained fixed upon the Apache's dark face. "Are you . . . are you going to scalp me too?" he croaked in a small voice.

Nantaje laughed. "No, I am not going to scalp you, little one. But I think I could get better hair than what that man back there gave me."

"It was the cream what done it."

"What cream?"

"The stuff my Uncle Alroy gave them back in Dixon last night."

"That was your uncle they killed?"

The boy nodded, and sniffed.

Nantaje thought he understood now. "Your uncle gave them something that made their hair fall out? And they came hunting him for revenge?"

Another small nod.

"What is your name?"

"Darby. Darby Gallagher. But everybody calls me Cubby."

"Cubby? It sounds like a child's name. I watched you fight to save your uncle. You deserve a warrior's name."

"A warrior's name?"

"Yes. I will call you War Hatchet because you attacked that man on the horse."

"I only used an iron skillet."

"Yes. But if you had a hatchet you would have used it, would you not?"

Cubby thought a moment. "I reckon so."

"Good. If I give over the reins to the horse, you would follow me, War Hatchet? You would not try to run away?"

Cubby looked around himself, at the grass hills that seemed to roll away forever.

"Where are we going?"

"To join with my friends."

"Are your friends . . . Indians?" Cubby gulped.

"No. But they are good men anyway."

"What is your name, sir?"

"Nantaje."

Cubby tried it out for size, but the syllables befouled his tongue and the best he could manage was Nan-ta-kee. "I reckon I ain't got no place to go to."

33

Nantaje swung off his saddle, adjusted the stirrups on Cubby's horse up to the last notch, then handed the reins over to the lad. "Follow me."

John Russell Keane spotted the two riders while they were still far off and pointed them out to the one-armed man riding to his left. "Looks like Nantaje has found himself a stray."

Royden Louvel narrowed his eyes toward the distant riders. "A mighty small stray." His soft southern accent was a sharp contrast to Keane's clipped northern words.

Dougal O'Brian scowled. "Just what we need. Another one." His gaze circled the small group. "We're becoming a mighty crowd, we are. Aye, and crowds make me nervous," he said, a touch of the old world still upon his tongue. Forty years this side of the Atlantic had sanded most of the rough edges smooth so that you hardly noticed the county Cork accent anymore, except whenever O'Brian got agitated.

"And why did you look at me like that just then?" Lionel shot back, his dark eyes glinting in the sunlight. The tall black man was the most recent outcast to have joined up with them. He leaned forward in his saddle and gave the Irishman a burning stare.

"I didn't look to you in particular," O'Brian replied. "I looked at everyone just the same." He chewed his dry lips and scratched at the beard that half hid the old brand upon his ruddy cheeks.

"You two lay off each other," Harrison Ridere said, moving his horse between them. "Let's hear what Nantaje's got to say before we go jumping the gun."

"I don't need a whippersnapper like you telling me what to do," O'Brian growled.

Ridere grinned at the older man. "You must have

34

run out of tequila again. You only get cranky when you've not had a drink, Dougal."

Keane considered each of them and gave a small shake of his head. Sometimes he wondered what kept them all together. But he knew the answer to that. If they didn't have each other, who else would they have—who else would want them? For the time being . . . at least until they reached California . . . they'd stick. This wasn't so much different than when he was commanding a company of men, he decided. Except back then he had held the rank of major. The men *had* to follow his orders. This loose collection of outcasts followed no one's orders but their own. Keane was always careful not to forget that.

When Nantaje and the boy arrived the men drew rein and circled around. The boy peered back at them, apprehension in his young face.

"Found him back along the trail, John Russell," Nantaje said to Keane. "He had been traveling with his uncle but they were waylaid along the road. They killed the uncle. The boy's name is War Hatchet."

"War Hatchet?" Keane frowned.

"Most people just call me Cubby," the boy said quickly, glancing at Nantaje.

"I named him War Hatchet for his courage."

"I see. If these men killed your uncle, how did you manage to escape?" Keane asked.

Again Cubby glanced at Nantaje. The Apache gave them the story, Cubby filling in the blank places. When they had finished, Keane said, "Lucky thing you were nearby, Nantaje." He considered the boy. "So you're orphaned now?"

Cubby nodded, fighting back his emotions.

"Well, yo' done found yoreself de right company

to keep, Cubby," Lionel declared. "We am all orphans—in a manner of speaking."

"Indeed, we *are* all orphaned," Louvel said with feeling. Keane knew the southerner was referring to something bigger than the loss of a mother and father.

"You have kin anywhere?" Keane asked.

Cubby hesitated. "I have an aunt who lives in Jack's Fork. Uncle Alroy was taking me there when those bad men stopped us."

"Then she will be expecting you. She'll be worried sick if you don't show."

"I don't think so, sir. You see, she didn't know I was coming out to live with her." His eyes dipped and his voice lowered. "Aunt Doreen and my ma, well, they didn't write much. She doesn't even know that my ma and pa are dead. Uncle Alroy, he sees Aunt Doreen from time to time in his travels—he was a peddler. He said the traveling way of life was not good for me so he was a-taking me to live with her when those men—" He couldn't bring himself to say it yet. His voice cracked and he dragged his sleeve across his eyes.

"I understand," Keane said.

"What are we to do with you, young man?" Louvel asked.

Cubby shrugged. "I don't know, sir."

Keane said, "Don't see that we have much choice. We'll take you on into Jack's Fork. It's only a little way northeast of here."

"And California is a far piece to the west of here," Dougal O'Brian pointed out grumpily.

"Ah don't see where this diversion will cost us much of a delay. The Union Pacific Railroad runs right through Jack's Fork, if my memory serves me right."

"Your memory serves you just fine, Captain Louvel," Keane said. "We can catch the train in Jack's Fork as easily as any other place along the line."

"Maybe even easier," Cubby said. "The railroad has got a big freight office there in Jack's Fork. My Uncle Horace Taylor, before he died, he used to run the place."

O'Brian scowled. "I suppose the detour won't matter much if that be the case."

"Ah'll wager that Jack's Fork has a fair amount of saloons too," Louvel added, giving the Irishman a look.

That brightened O'Brian's face some. "Well, in that case, we ought to take the lad to his aunt," O'Brian allowed, dragging a tongue along his dry lips.

Harrison Ridere was eyeing the two haunches of meat hanging across the back of Nantaje's horse. "Before we go anywhere I'm for roasting up some of that antelope and filling this hole in my belly."

Here was something they could all agree on.

Amongst a small stand of cottonwoods near a creek, they built a fire and cooked. Afterward, with the afternoon drawing long in the tooth and the men feeling full and contented, they decided to make camp for the night, planning to reach Jack's Fork about midmorning the next day.

Cubby had a hard time falling asleep as he thought over all that had happened. These strangers seemed nice enough, but would they really take him to his aunt? And what of that Indian? A dozen different worries churned inside his head. He'd heard stories of boys being murdered in their sleep by wild Indians. Cubby watched the blankets where the Apache slept. He'd have to keep an eye on him all night.

But the strain of the day was catching up with him. His eyelids were heavy and his thoughts turned back to his Uncle Alroy. Suddenly he saw the faces of those men again, of Kersten's scarred visage glaring at him. The vision startled him awake and he realized he had been dreaming.

Settling down again, Cubby rested his head upon his folded arms and was fast asleep.

Burl Rahn was hardly aware of how busy the Iron Rail Saloon was at this late hour as he stared at the half-drunk glass of whiskey clutched in his fingers. Langston and Brawley were slumped in their chairs across the table from him, their heads buzzing from drink but their moods stone-cold sober. Of the three, only Kleef Langston had not plowed into the whiskey as soon as his feet had hit town. He'd taken his time at it, trying to keep a clear head, and an eye on the batwing doors. But Langston did not expect the law to come looking for them—not yet at least. Not until that peddler wagon was discovered and what remained of Alroy Gallagher had been found among its ashes. It was just as likely no one would ever come looking.

"Maybe we should have trailed them Injuns, Burl?" Cooper Brawley said finally, putting words to the concern that weighed heavy on their minds.

"And do what when we caught up with them?" Rahn shoved his fingers through what remained of his hair. "Already lost enough of this. I've no desire to give the rest over to them scalping redskins."

Brawley slumped deeper into his chair. "I don't know, Burl. Maybe we should never have taken out after that drummer in the first place."

Langston looked away from the batwing doors. "I say we head back to the ranch and work our jobs like nothing ever happened. Make up some story about how Lars got fed up with it all and took off on his own, or maybe he found himself a woman and left with her. We say nothing about this ever again. In a few weeks, a few months, it would all be history. If that peddler's body is ever found, no one will connect it to us. Especially if we don't make a fuss about this." He briefly lifted his hat to reveal his molting head, then hurriedly tugged it back down.

Rahn tapped his glass upon the table, thinking it over.

"Kleef's got a point, Burl," Brawley said. "If we stay clean for a while, nobody will ever finger us for that murder."

"You're forgetting about them Injuns. They must have seen everything that happened."

"So what if they did? What are a pack of murdering Injuns going to do about it?" Langston asked. "Turn us in to the law? Not on your life. They won't do a thing. They've likely already drifted on down into Colorado by now. No, I think Cooper's right."

"And that kid?"

"The Injuns took him. He won't be talking to no one for a long time, if ever again," Kleef said confidently.

Rahn grunted, tossed back his whiskey and banged the glass down on the table. "What will the boys say when we come back to the ranch looking like half-shorn sheep? Got to spin them some kind of yarn about how it happened."

"We'll think of something," Brawley said. "We got all day tomorrow to work on it."

Rahn thought it over, warming to the plan after a bit. He lowered his voice so as not to be heard beyond their table. "It's about all we can do, boys. Like

Kleef says, we'll just lay low and keep our mouths shut. We can claim Kersten got a hankering to see other places and up and left, promising to send a letter to the outfit when he gets to wherever it is he's going, telling the boss where to send any pay owed to him."

"That will go over fine," Brawley allowed. "All we got to do is come up with a good story for our—" He hesitated. "Our affliction."

Just then the batwings slammed open. In strode a bosomy woman wearing a loose-fitting grimy blouse drawn tight at her thick waist by a broad, black holster belt with the scuffed butt of a Remington revolver thrust forward in cross-draw fashion. The men gave way as her heavy boots thumped up to the bar. She reached deep into the pocket of her trousers and fished out a coin, clanging it down on the bar.

"Why, if it ain't Patty!" the barman declared.

"I need whiskey, Sam, and you best leave the bottle."

"You look all a-fluster, Patty. What happened?" the bartender asked, concerned.

"After you see what I got out front in my wagon, you'll know why." She filled a glass and drank it down at once. "Looks like we are fixing to have us some trouble, Sam," Patty said. She faced the room and bellowed, "Injun trouble, boys."

The chatter died down. Over at their table, Rahn, Brawley and Langston perked up.

"What are you talking about, Patty?" someone in the saloon asked.

She eyed the man like a marksman taking aim. "Come along with me, Frank Cleary, and I'll show you just what I mean." Patty slugged back a shot of whiskey, sleeved a dribble from her chin and marched for the doors, slamming them apart with both hands. A crowd of curious men trailed after her, Rahn and his friends among them.

Out front in the street loomed the dark bulk of a freight wagon, its six mules shifting impatiently, flicking their tails, stomping a hoof now and again. Patty slapped one of the animals on the rump and said, "Patience, deary. I'm just gonna show these folks what we found, then it's off for some hay and water."

She went around back, unhooked a chain, lifted a heavy latch and swung the gate wide. Reaching inside the dark maw of the freighter, Patty gave a grunt and heaved out the body of a man and dropped it at the feet of them standing there.

"I was bringing a load up from Dixon when I spied the smoking remains of a burned-out wagon in the middle of the road. Looks like it had been ransacked pretty good. I got to looking around and found this unfortunate fellow off the road a piece."

Some of the men bent for a closer look.

"Why, this feller's been scalped!" one of them said, shooting to his feet and backing away as if the condition might somehow prove contagious.

"I'll say it again," Patty growled. "Looks like we might be heading for some trouble."

"Injuns around here have been mostly peaceful for years," a voice among them noted and there ensued a worried discussion on the matter.

Rahn moved through the crowd for a closer look. His expression remained guarded until he had moved off a little way with Langston and Brawley. "That takes care of our problem."

"How do you figure?" Brawley asked quietly.

"Don't you see? It was Injuns that attacked and burned that wagon, and Injuns what murdered that

41

peddler and Kersten. No one is even going to suspect us now."

Langston was grinning. "Couldn't have worked out better if we'd planned it that way."

"Someone better go for Sheriff Peterson," Patty said, swinging the wagon's tailgate shut and threading a chain through the latch. She brushed her hands together. "I've done my part for the poor soul. Now, I need me another drink before I haul my asses down to the livery!"

The crowd parted as Patty went back inside the saloon.

Chapter Four

They came into Jack's Fork from the south. It was a rawboned railroading town, given over mostly to the booming business of the U.P., but there were hints here and there of other enterprises flourishing side by side with the great transcontinental monopoly. A mining supply warehouse reminded Keane of the years he'd spent down in Tombstone scratching for silver on his own claim. That was right after his "retirement" from the army—at least he called it his retirement. He'd been forced out of the army, and that still galled him.

Keane shoved the memory back where he kept such things. His view moved up the rutted road, past a long string of cattle pens along the U.P. tracks. There were no cows in them at present, but judging from their size, there must be a growing cattle concern in this part of the Wyoming Territory as well.

Jack's Fork held an assortment of the usual boomtown businesses. There was even a church, prominent by its tall steeple, standing on the next street over. A general store, a millinery shop, a jeweler, a lawyer, a gunsmith, all lined the main street. There was a large hardware store too, and a fire department, a dry goods store and a meat market, even a combined real estate, insurance and loan business. He noted two banks among the mix along with four or five saloons and billiard rooms.

"This wasn't a half-bad notion after all," O'Brian admitted, eyeing a saloon across the way.

"We might want to spend a day or two here," Louvel suggested, touching his vest where Keane knew the one-armed gambler kept a deck of playing cards in an inside pocket.

Nantaje's dark eyes surveyed the town, reading the faces of the people who stopped on the boardwalks to watch this collection of strangers ride in. They seemed particularly intent upon him. "You'd think they have never seen an Apache before, John Russell."

"This far north, most haven't."

Nantaje grunted. "I don't like this place."

"We won't stay," Keane said. "Only long enough to get Cubby squared away with his aunt."

Cubby rode alongside them, his short legs bowed across the wide back of the horse. Even with the stirrups as high as they could go, his shoes barely reached inside them.

"What is your Aunt Doreen's last name?" Keane asked.

"It's Taylor, sir."

"We shouldn't have any trouble locating her," Keane said.

They turned into a hitching rail in front of the sheriff's office and dismounted. O'Brian's feet started automatically toward the nearest saloon, and as they did he snagged hold of Ridere's shirt sleeve. "Harry and me are gonna just check out this here watering hole."

Ridere grinned. "Looks like I'm going with him," and the two of them aimed for the open door.

Louvel shook his head. "Ah declare if those two aren't a pair of peas in a pod. Drinking and women are all they have on their brains. You'd think Harry at least would have learned his lesson."

"Some men never learn," Keane said. "Well, let's go see if we can find this Doreen Taylor."

"I think I will wait out here," Nantaje said.

Keane glanced up at the shingle over the door. "The law makes you nervous?"

"This town makes me nervous, John Russell. I like it better out here in the open where I can keep an eye on things. War Hatchet will wait with me."

The boy was clearly torn, but in the end he nodded.

"I'll stay with them too," Lionel said. "My last run-in with de law got me a rope around my neck. I still ain't got over de feel of dat."

Keane said, "All right. Captain Louvel and I will be right back."

Rahn felt vaguely queasy in the stomach and his head throbbed like a skin drum. Brawley wasn't feeling much better either, and even Langston, who had been careful with his drinking, was moving sluggishly this morning, sporting bloodshot eyes and carrying an insatiable thirst. Coffee didn't help much. It was water they drank mostly over breakfast in the Express Café. The eggs and ham helped a little too. They had gotten hardly any sleep, and what little they had managed was full of fits and starts as

45

the whiskey worked its way out of their blood.

"Celebrating like we done last night can do a man in," Brawley noted.

After breakfast they had another cup of coffee and pondered the merits of the temperance movement and the demands of the W.C.T.U., deciding in the end that prohibition really was bad for the country— in spite of their present condition.

"As much as I'm not looking forward to the ride, I'm afraid it's time to get back to the ranch before we lose our jobs," Rahn said finally.

On the sidewalk outside the morning sun seared their eyes. They tugged their hats down low, keeping their eyes bent to the ground as they started for their horses. Langston shoved a boot into the stirrup and had started up into his saddle when he happened to glance across the street. He stopped midway.

"Burl!"

"What?" Rahn asked impatiently.

"Across the street, in front of the sheriff's office. You better take a look."

Rahn and Brawley turned.

"It's the kid!" Rahn hissed, careful to keep his voice low.

"It can't be." Brawley squinted hard.

"And look what's with him," Langston said. "That's an Injun if I ever seen one."

"The other one ain't," Brawley said, still sounding like he wasn't going to believe his eyes.

"Let's get out of sight." They mounted up and rode to the end of town, drawing up behind some warehouses of the U.P.

"Think he saw us?" Brawley asked.

"Didn't look like he did," Langston answer. "This sure enough is gonna throw a wrench in our clockworks."

"Shut up and let me think!" Rahn hopped to the ground and began pacing back and forth along a weedy section of unused track.

Brawley and Langston dismounted too, Brawley peering around the corner and up the street. Langston built himself a cigarette and took a seat upon an old pile of creosoted ties to smoke it.

"Doesn't look like he spied us," Brawley said.

Langston handed him his pouch and papers. "Fix yourself a smoke."

"Thanks."

Rahn came over, worry lines cut deep into his forehead. "So much for the notion that they drifted down into Colorado," he said, narrowing an eye at Langston.

"Okay, so I was wrong. The question is, what are we going to do about it?"

"Only one thing to do."

"If you're thinking about knocking the kid off, I don't like it."

Brawley began to shake his head. "I don't like it either, Kleef, but I like it less knowing that kid is still alive to finger us for the ones who killed that peddler."

Rahn said, "Not only the kid, but that Injun too. It wouldn't surprise me if he was the one who done Kersten in."

Langston pulled the smoke into his lungs, held it a moment, then let it dribble out slow while he stared at the cigarette in his fingers. Resignation rang in his voice when he finally spoke. "How are we going to do it?"

Rahn shook his head. "Haven't figured it out yet. But one thing is certain, when we do it, we got to make sure that kid and that Injun are somewhere

47

where no one will see or hear. I won't make the same mistake twice, and that's the straight of it!"

Keane and Louvel emerged from the sheriff's office just as the blast of a steam whistle rolled up the street from the train station at the edge of town. Keane turned to the sound, saw the plume of black smoke billowing above the roofs. It was moving west. They could have been on it.

"There will be other trains, Major," Louvel said as if he knew what Keane was thinking.

"I know, Captain Louvel." Keane found it curious that he and Louvel persisted in referring to each other according to a rank each of them had left behind years ago. Louvel had come out of West Point a captain and had been immediately thrust into the war. Keane had moved up in rank by battlefield commissions. He'd finished the war a breveted colonel, but of course, those had been only temporary advancements and were practically meaningless after the war ended.

"Did the sheriff know where to find her?" Nantaje asked.

Cubby chewed his lip, waiting for the reply.

"Indeed," Keane said. He grinned down at Cubby. "It seems your aunt is a prominent lady about town. She lives at the end of Commerce Street. Sheriff says we can't miss it. Big house surrounded by a hedge and a wrought-iron fence, with the name 'Taylor' above the gate."

They found the house exactly where the sheriff said it would be, an imposing edifice of brick and white shingles, three stories high with a green copper roof. Gleaming black iron balconies circled the top floor, and a fire escape switchbacked down one side.

"Golly," Cubby breathed, his eyes feasting upon the groomed grounds, the white gazebo, the tree-lined carriage drive that circled around to the front of the house and beneath a porte cochere where a neat brick step-up waited to aid people into their coaches.

Louvel gave a quiet sigh. "This reminds me of my home back in New Orleans."

"Glory, don't it!" Lionel declared. "Will yo' look at all them windows."

"Reminds me of the governor's mansion back in Iowa," Keane replied.

"How many people live in this lodge?" Nantaje asked, more curious than awed.

"According to the sheriff, just Mrs. Taylor and two servants. He said the household used to be quite a bit larger before her husband died."

"I'm going to live here?" Cubby gushed.

"Sorta looks like it, partner." Keane dropped a big hand upon the boy's shoulder.

"Shall we make our introductions?" Louvel suggested.

They turned their horses onto the driveway, where crushed gravel crunched under their horses' hooves. Beneath the long awning that stretched across the drive they dismounted and tied up at iron rings spaced along a rail. There were eight steps to the porch that crossed the front of the house and bent around its sides. Perhaps it completely encircled the place, but Keane couldn't see beyond the two distant corners. The front door was a tall and wide affair of raised panels, painted a pale shade of blue, with a bright brass knocker right in the middle. Keane lifted the heavy ring and let it drop with a loud thump.

As they waited, Keane let his view travel out

across the grounds. From this angle the lawn appeared unkempt. "Looks like it's a lot for a widow woman to keep up," he noted.

Nantaje grunted and nodded. "Gophers make big holes all over yard."

"Sorta looks that way," Keane said. The yard was full of mounds where some animal had been digging. "Maybe she has problems with dogs."

Behind the door a latch moved and the wide plank gave a squeal as it swung slowly open. A young black woman in a black dress and white apron stood there. Her hair was drawn together and turned into a bun at the back of her head. Impatience pinched her face. "Yes? What is it?" she inquired.

Keane removed his hat. "We would like to see Mrs. Taylor."

The woman considered them in a glance, narrowing her eyes slightly and peering down her wide nose at Lionel. Her eyes lingered upon their trail-worn clothes and her mouth tightened. "If you are looking for work, you will have to speak to Charles. And he is not here at present."

Louvel said, "It is not work we are seeking, ma'am. It is the lady of the house we wish to speak to."

"Is Madam expecting you?" she asked, her eyes straying to the empty sleeve pinned up where Louvel's right arm had once been.

"We have just arrived in town."

"Madam Taylor accepts appointments only." The woman began to shut the door.

Keane put out a hand and stopped it. "I think she ought to see us this time—without the appointment."

She scowled at his hand blocking the door. "Why is that?" she said impatiently.

"Because, you see, this lad here is Cubby Gallagher."

"Cubby Gallagher?" The name appeared to mean nothing at first, and then the woman looked again, understanding coming suddenly to her eyes. "Darby Gallagher?"

"Yes, ma'am," Cubby said softly, worrying the brim of his tattered brown hat in his small fingers. "I come to live with my Aunt Doire—er, Aunt Doreen."

She was speechless for a moment as she absorbed this startling news. "I see. Just wait here a minute," and she shut the door.

"Now we will see some action," Louvel said confidently.

They waited three or four minutes before the sound of approaching footsteps grew louder on the other side of the door. It swung open with more energy this time and a woman in a blue, satiny dress was standing there. Mrs. Doreen Taylor was stunningly attractive, mid to late forties and quite slender. Her hair was very black with streaks of gray running through it, and her eyes were brown. Her fair complexion bespoke a woman who was careful never to venture out of doors without a parasol. Her lips showed the faintest tint of color, and at the moment they were pulled tight together in a perturbed frown as she looked first at Keane, then down at Cubby.

"Mrs. Taylor?"

"I am Doreen Taylor. Who are you?" The muted southern accent did little to blunt the sharp edge in her retort.

"My name is John Keane and these are my friends. We found this lad out on the trail. He's been orphaned and his uncle was bringing him here to live with you. I reckon you are his only remaining kin now."

She glanced briefly at the five of them before her view settled upon Cubby. "Are you Darby?" she asked.

"I am."

"Your mother is dead?"

Keane marveled at her complete lack of remorse at the news of her sister's death. He noticed that Louvel's face held a strangely puzzled look.

"Yes, ma'am. So's my pa. A fire burned down our house and took 'em away to heaven, ma'am."

"And what of Alroy?"

"He was bringing me here to you, but we got set upon by highwaymen and he was killed."

Keane saw a sudden change come to Louvel's face. His eyes were slowly widening, his mouth slightly agape, and Keane wondered if he was feeling ill.

Doreen Taylor appeared at a loss as to what to do next. Keane figured inviting them inside would be a proper first step, and she must have thought of it too just then. "You all better come in," she said. "Christine, please bring tea."

"Yes, Madam." The servant departed.

"Well, come in, come in," she said, stepping aside for them. "Don't want the neighbors to start to talk."

They followed Doreen Taylor inside—all but Louvel, who didn't move. His face had gone solid now, like chiseled stone, and his fingers had crushed the crown of his hat against his chest. Doreen Taylor led them into a great room that was about three times the size of any parlor Keane had ever entered.

Keane turned back and said quietly, "Are you coming, Captain Louvel."

At his words, Doreen stopped dead in her tracks,

her back suddenly stiff as a flagpole. Slowly she turned back and stared at Louvel.

Louvel gulped a couple times.

Doreen's eyes widened.

"Doireann?" he croaked.

"Royden?" she breathed, her face drained and pale as baking soda.

He nodded.

Doreen Taylor fainted straightaway.

Chapter Five

They carried the mistress of the house to a settee while Christine bustled off to the kitchen for a glass of water. Louvel cooled Doreen Taylor's flushed face with a paper fan from a nearby end table.

In a few moments Doreen's eyes fluttered open and with the aid of Christine she sat up and sipped from a crystal glass the maid put to her lips. Then she pushed the glass aside and stared up at Louvel.

"Royden, is that really you?"

Louvel was recovering from the shock too. "It is Ah, Doireann. Ah . . . ," he hesitated. "Ah must say, Ah never thought Ah would ever see you again, although hardly a week or a month went by when you weren't on my mind. That last day, upon the porch swing at your daddy's house, before Ah went off to West Point—the memory is indelibly marked upon my brain."

"Mine as well," she replied, staring as if she had

54

seen the dead resurrected. "I was wearing a peach chiffon dress, and you were in that black frock you always wore when you traveled."

He smiled at the memory her words brought back to him. "Ah recall it. Charles served us juleps, and Ah fussed because he had not included the bourbon."

"But I was only sixteen, if you remember."

"How could Ah forget? Ah was only two years your senior, off to join the army. Ah felt so grown up."

"We were both young and silly. Oh, Royden." Sadness filling her voice. "All the years we missed. What happened to you? After the war I looked. I spoke with Howie Munster and he put the word out to all the boys coming home. Then one day a young man arrived at the house I was staying in—the Radcliffs, you remember them, don't you?"

Louvel nodded. "Like the rest of us, they lost everything."

Doreen nodded. "But they were determined to stay and rebuild." Her eyes glazed and she reached for a handkerchief. "The young man said he had word of you, that you had been killed at Old Cold Harbor."

Louvel gave a small nod. "It was at the Battle of Gaines's Mill. Ah was a captain in D. H. Hill's division when we advanced against Sykes to the east of Old Cold Harbor. That was when Ah lost this to Yankee grapeshot." Louvel lifted the stump of his right arm. "Ah nearly bled to death on the battlefield, but Ah was found and taken to a surgeon, then later moved to a field hospital north of Old Cold Harbor. Afterward, Ah was shuffled around some, and finally ended up in a hospital in Richmond. Ah spent most of that year recuperating, then Ah was moved some more, but always the damned Yankees were right there, and we had to move again. It is easy to see how the rumor of my death might have begun.

"Eventually Ah found myself on the coast, at Fort Fisher serving under Colonel Lamb. Ah was a lookout for federal blockades. It was about the only service Ah could render, still recovering from my wound as Ah was. Ah remained there until Fort Fisher fell in 1865. By then the war was almost over. Afterward, Ah made my way back to New Orleans, but the place was so overrun with northern vermin that Ah had to move on. Ah tarried there only long enough to view the burned-out ruins of my home. Ah've been traveling ever since."

When he finished, Doreen reached out and took his hand. "But now you are back."

"Now Ah am back," Louvel said.

Just then an old black man came down a hallway from the back of the house. He entered the parlor, half surprised to see all of them standing there. His hair was white as frost on a windowpane, and his face wrinkled and gaunt. He walked stiffly, as if his bones no longer wanted to move for him.

"Sorry, Miss Doreen," he said upon seeing that he had interrupted them. "I didn't know you had visitors."

"That's all right," she began.

"Charles?" Louvel blurted.

The old man stared, his eyes slowly widening. "Why, is that Mr. Loo-vel? No, it can't be. Not unless you am done climbed up out of the grave!"

"It is, and Ah feel like Ah have climbed out of a grave, Charles."

The old man hobbled over for a closer look. "Why, it is you!"

"Charles never left me," Doreen said. "After the

war, neither of us had any place to go."

"I took care of missy when she was but a babe, I did. And I am still taking care of her!" Charles said proudly.

After the initial rush of excitement, Doreen calmed down and drew composure around her like a comforting quilt, once more taking command.

She peered at Cubby. Her eyebrows moved briefly together, her lips compressing. "Christine, prepare one of the rooms on the third floor for young Mr. Gallagher."

"Yes, Madam."

"Go with Christine, Darby."

Cubby hesitated, peering up the long staircase.

"War Hatchet," Nantaje said dropping to his haunches at the boy's side. "You will be all right here. I will come back to make sure all is well."

Cubby nodded and reached for Christine's hand. The servant pulled it out of his reach and started up the stairs.

Lionel frowned. He and Nantaje exchanged glances. Nantaje said to Doreen Taylor, "You will give War Hatchet care?"

"War Hatchet?" she asked, making it sound like she had just bitten into a lemon.

"It is his warrior name."

Her face pinched around the mouth. "I will see that *Darby* is properly managed," Doreen replied coolly.

Keane's view was on the old black house servant. Charles seemed worried about something, trying to hide the impatience. The man clearly had something important he wanted to tell Mrs. Taylor, but was refraining from mentioning it now with all of them there.

Doreen Taylor turned back to Louvel, a sudden

smile erasing the scowling lines from her forehead. "You must join me for dinner tonight, Royden." Then she remembered the others. "You and your friends, of course," she added woodenly, a flash of consternation leaping to her face as she glanced at Lionel and Nantaje.

Louvel was too moonstruck to catch it.

Kcane said, "We thank you for the invite, ma'am, but you and Captain Louvel have a lot of catching up to do. We'd only be a fifth wheel on the cart if we tagged along. I wouldn't want us to get in the way."

Doreen did not insist.

Keane said, "We've disrupted your day enough as it is. I think my friends and I will be going now— now that Cubby is in good hands."

Louvel dragged himself from his romantic trance and said, "Yes, we must go for now."

"Seven o'clock?"

"Seven o'clock will be perfect," he said, then he looked down at his dusty attire and frowned.

Cubby was nowhere in sight and Keane said, "Tell Cubby we will be back to see him before we leave town."

Doreen merely nodded and followed them out onto the porch. She took Louvel's hand one last time. "We do have so much catching up to do, Royden."

He bowed gallantly and said, "Until this evening." Turning stiffly away, Louvel donned his hat and descended the wide steps to their waiting horses.

They rode out of the drive onto the street and Lionel said, "I'm thinking Mr. Cubby am gonna have hisself a rough ride with dat outfit."

Louvel looked over, his serene smile faltering a bit. "What do you mean by that? It will be a wonderful place for him to live."

Lionel looked skeptical. "I seen more joy in a graveyard than I did on the face of dat servant, Christine. And de house marm—she wants dat chil' about as much as I wants a dose of scarlet fever. I seen it all over her when Mr. John told her why we come." Lionel bobbed his head a couple times. "Yes, sir, Mr. Cubby's in for a rough ride."

"Suh, you are impertinent!" Louvel declared hotly.

"Imper'nent? And yo' am too blinded by yore heart to see de truth, Mr. Royden."

"You take care to watch your words. Ah'll not have you defaming Mrs. Taylor that way."

"My, am we getting uppity of a sudden. I is only saying what am clear to anyone with eyes!"

Louvel reined to a stop and glared at the black man. "Ah don't need to hear a lecture from you, boy."

Lionel stiffened. "And yo' won't be getting one." He heeled his horse ahead and rode into town, leaving them standing there.

"I figured it was coming," Keane said.

"What?" Louvel snapped, twisting around in his saddle.

"You and Lionel."

Louvel screwed up his lips and exhaled sharply through his nose. "There was a time in my life when impertinence like that would have been followed by bucking and a good whipping."

"You seem to be forgetting that that time is past. That world you remember so fondly no longer exists, Captain Louvel."

"Ah haven't forgotten, Major Keane. Ah have never forgotten what you and others like you have done to me and my country! What you have taken away."

59

"There comes a time to bury the past. You could have rebuilt all that you lost, if you had wanted to." Keane nodded toward the big house. "She obviously did."

"Ah don't need to hear a lecture from you as well, Major."

"Then get rid of that chip you're carrying and daring everyone to knock off. What happened twenty years ago happened. Accept that."

"Ah shall never accept that." Louvel chucked his horse forward, sitting straight and proud in the saddle as he rode away.

Keane found Nantaje staring at him. "Well?"

Nantaje shrugged. "I do not understand all that he speaks of. But I know one thing. Lionel see truth with his eyes."

Keane grimaced. "Lionel sees it, I see it, you see it . . . but Louvel? All Louvel sees is what is past."

"It is this war you two speak of? The one between the North and South? It has left deep wounds, has it not?"

"Wounds that may never heal if folks refuse to stop living in the past."

"In this war, who was right and who was wrong?"

Keane shook his head. "There were legitimate grievances on both sides. But as to who was right and who was wrong? Well, that's a question historians will be working on for the next hundred years. Come on, let's go see if we can find our two pouting friends."

"John Russell." Nantaje lowered his voice. His suddenly wary eyes sent a prickling up Keane's spine.

"What is it?"

"Don't look right away. On the corner is a man. He was standing there when we rode up. He watched us go to the big lodge. He is watching us now, but he holds a paper in front of himself to hide his stealth."

Keane stole a glance. "I'm not surprised we drew attention to ourselves, considering the scene we just made here in the middle of the road."

"No, I think there is more to it than that."

Keane rode his horse in a circle, as if merely to come around to the other side of Nantaje. As he did he got a good look at the man whose face was mostly hidden behind an open newspaper. He was no taller than average and wore a fawn-colored suit with wide pinstripes, and a black bowler hat. Keane could not see the face, but his shoulders filled out the jacket and his big chest pulled at the buttons that fastened it in front while his arms pushed at its sleeves.

"He watched us leave the lodge too, and there was the look of a hunter in his eyes."

"Hum. Why would he be interested in us?"

Nantaje shook his head. "Maybe he is stalking the woman, Taylor?"

"Or maybe just waiting for a friend."

"I will keep an eye open, John Russell. I do not like leaving War Hatchet in that big lodge with those people."

Keane grinned. "You've sure taken a shine to the kid."

"He reminds me of Tejon."

"Your sister's son?"

Nantaje nodded. "Someday Tejon will be a mighty warrior. And so will War Hatchet. He has a warrior spirit. I saw that when those men attacked."

Keane glanced back again to see the newspaper suddenly hide the man's face. "He is sort of shy about showing his face, isn't he?" Keane said. "You just might be right."

"Christine, come down here," Doreen Taylor called from the foyer.

Up on the third floor, the servant turned toward the open door, then looked quickly at Cubby. "This will be your room for now. You can open those windows to let a breeze in, but mind you, best not climb out onto that fire escape. Madam will likely whale the tar out of you if you do." Christine lifted her eyebrows and stared down at him, her large owl eyes unblinking, her tight lips stern and unsmiling.

"Yes, ma'am," he said.

"Christine!"

"Coming, Madam," she said hurrying out the door. Cubby listened to her receding feet pounding the staircase, doing double time upon the treads until the echo of them reaching the marble landing sounded like a loud clap.

He looked around the place. The room was cozy and very feminine, from the walls papered with yellow daisies, to the carpet of red and yellow flowers. There was an elegant bedstead and a dressing table holding a blue and white china pitcher and bowl. The bed covering was all of white lace, and when he sat upon it he sank comfortably into a thick feather mattress. There were paintings in gilded frames upon the walls, mostly of women in pretty dresses and gentlemen wearing suits, like folks going to a picnic in someone's garden, with lots of flowers all around and the people's faces painted with no details. The women seemed too tall, the men too sissy-looking for Cubby's liking.

He raised the window sash and peered out across the yard. There was most of an acre, he reckoned, all boxed in with that wrought-iron fencing and stands of shrubs, mostly trimmed up to look like they had flat sides. There was a carriage house, a water pump and a toolshed tucked away in one corner near a flower garden. Looking the grounds over, Cubby saw the grass was in terrible shape, with little mounds of overturned dirt scattered about like his Aunt Doireann had a bad infestation of gophers. Just below him ran an iron balcony that ended at some iron stairs. The fire escape Christine had warned him about. Beyond the fence to the right and left stood more houses, none as large as his aunt's place.

He heard voices and thrust his head farther out the open window. In the next yard over a plump boy about his own age, with reddish face and brown slicked-down hair, and wearing knickers, was chasing a wheel with a stick. A white and black dog romped at his side.

Cubby pulled back inside and as he was ogling the room he caught the sound of voices wafting softly up from the parlor far below. He went out into the hall and looked over the banister. The main floor was dizzyingly far away. His stomach made a leap and he stepped back with a shiver of fright.

"—as if I don't have enough problems," he heard his aunt say.

"What should I tell him next time he comes around?" Charles's husky voice asked. "This is the second time he come by asking to be paid. He says he fixed the wheel and put on a new axle and it cost most of twenty-five dollars."

"I don't know. Tell him I'll pay him next week. Make some excuse. I don't know. I'm under the weather, that's it. Tell him as soon as I'm back on my feet I'll be round to pay the bill." Her voice sounded strained.

Then Christine said, "And he's not the only one, Madam. Mr. Kettleridge asked me when you was going to settle up on that bill at the store. I said I'd tell you about it."

"When it rain it pours," Doreen lamented. "Not only do I have these creditors breathing down my back, but now I have that . . . that kid upstairs! My sister and her worthless husband get themselves killed, her brother-in-law gets murdered and I'm stuck with a ten-year-old brat to raise. Whatever am I going to do?"

Charles said, "It'll be nice having a young one about the place, Miss Doreen. Why, I remember when it was you and your sis about the house and I would take the two of you down to the river and teach you how to snag for them catfish. Remember? Why, that was a grand old time, yes, it surely was. Remember when we would drive into town to collect your pappy's mail, or a delivery for your mam?" Charles's deep voice chuckled. "Having Master Darby about will do this old man good."

"Well, it won't do this lady any good," Doreen's voice cut in bitterly, then lowered as if the walls had ears and she wanted what she was about to say kept from them. "Besides, you know what we have to do here. How can we with *him* around?"

"Master Darby can help us with that, Miss Doreen," Charles said.

"Master Darby will blab his fool mouth off," Doreen retorted. "That's the way kids are. No, Master Darby will have to go."

"Go?" Charles sounded concerned. "But where? The boy's an orphan."

64

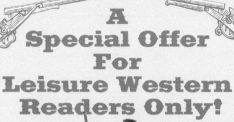

Get Four Books Totally
F R E E* —
A Value between
$16 and $20

Tear here and mail your FREE* book card today!

PLEASE RUSH
MY FOUR FREE*
BOOKS TO ME
RIGHT AWAY!

LeisureWestern Book Club
P.O. Box 6613
Edison, NJ 08818-6613

Christine said, "Isn't there an orphanage in Cheyenne?"

"Yes, of course," Doreen said, "the orphanage. You must write a letter today, Christine. Find its name, and address the letter to the headmaster. Tell him we will be bringing in an orphan."

"When will we be arriving? He'll want to know that."

"I don't know. Soon. After those men who brought him here leave town."

"And what of Mr. Loo-vel?" Charles asked.

Doreen's voice softened. "Royden. How could I have forgotten?"

"I seen the look in his eyes, Miss Doreen. I don't think Mr. Loo-vel will be leaving with those others."

"No, of course not," Doreen said. "I lost that man once. I don't intend to lose him again."

"And what of our task here?"

"He'll have to be told, eventually. He'll understand, I know he will."

"I hope you are right, Miss Doreen," Charles replied. "And Master Darby, he will understand too, if we don't go and send him away."

"No. Absolutely not. The last thing I need is a runny-nose brat cluttering up my life. Darby will have to go!"

Up at the top of the stairs, Cubby wiped away the moisture that had begun to run down his cheeks. It was as he had feared in spite of all his Uncle Alroy's words. His Uncle Alroy hadn't wanted to be bothered either. No one wanted him.

Coming to a decision, Cubby returned to the bedroom, shut the door behind him and crawled out the open window onto the iron ledge. The ground through the open latticework beneath his feet seemed a long way down and again a sudden dizziness made him clutch to the handrail. Far below him was a patch of worked ground that looked like a flower bed. But the flowers were faring poorly and the garden was mostly brown and weedy. Overhead, the roof dipped down so low that Cubby could almost reach a hand up to the gutters. He clearly saw the copper sheathing, green like moss growing all over it, only he knew it wasn't moss. It was just the way copper looked after years of weathering.

He made his way along the narrow balcony to the steps. They were all open ironwork too and the ground wavered frighteningly far below him. The boy in the yard next door was gone. Beyond the fence and shrubs a stream lined with cottonwood trees cut past the property. Scrubbing the tears from his eyes, Cubby clutched his way down those terrifying steps that zigzagged alongside the house until with a great sigh of relief his feet landed upon solid ground.

He dashed across the gopher-plagued yard, up and over the fence and plunged down the slope to the stream. Tears clouded his view as he ran and sobs caught in his throat and rattled his chest. He ran headlong with no idea where he was going. It didn't matter to him so long as it was away from that horrible house.

He'd never be a burden to grown-ups again.

Chapter Six

Cubby hadn't gone but a hundred yards when, through the glaze of his grief, he saw that he had left the last of the houses behind and was following the small waterway out onto open prairie. Cottonwoods still crowded the stream bank, but they had begun to thin some here. Cubby slowed the pace of his blind retreat from his aunt's house, suddenly wary. His shoulders tightened, a tingle ran up his spine, and he stopped, all at once afraid. Panting and trying to catch his breath, his hearing was momentarily muted by the thumping of his heart and the blood pounding in his ears. He made out the quiet ripple of water flowing to his left and a bird or two scolding somewhere overhead . . . and that was all.

He put his back to a tree trunk and dragged a sleeve across his eyes, scrubbing them dry. There was a faint odor of smoke in the air, but Cubby didn't think anything of it right then. Other thoughts were bubbling to the surface of his brain. He was suddenly realizing that if he did leave, he'd have to make his own way in the world. Other boys had done so at his age. He could too, he determined.

He might hop a train and ride it back East where the land was more settled and there would be opportunities for a boy to make out. Or he might snatch a ride on a westbound, and try the adventurous life? That didn't appeal to him very much. There were still plenty of wild Indians about, and he'd rather not run across anymore. The next one might not be so friendly as Nan-ta-kee.

East, he decided. That's where he would go. Cubby knew little about how the railroads ran except that the Union Pacific had a junction in Cheyenne that went south, to Denver. He had friends in Denver City. There was Petey Ross who lived three houses down from where Cubby used to live, and Jacob Rice Boone who was only two streets over from him. That's what he would do. Hop a train to Cheyenne, and another to Denver. His plan laid out, Cubby stood away from the tree and tried to get his bearings, but there wasn't much he could see down alongside the stream. The railroad yards lay to his left, he figured, and that was the place to start.

The wind changed just then and the smoke from a nearby campfire wafted down from a wooded ledge above. There was the crack of a twig underfoot. Cubby's spine went rigid again, and now he heard the not so distant nicker of a horse. He turned to hurry away from there, when all at once a heavy hand came down upon his shoulder and a gruff voice declared, "Well, what do we have here?"

He spun around, his heart leaping to his throat. "Startled you, did I?"

She was a big woman, with a sunburned face beneath a wide hat, like a man might wear. Her skin was leather tough, crisscrossed with deep creases. From two folds of skin, bright blue eyes sparkled like chunks of polished turquoise. Cubby stared in spite of himself. She wore a grimy blue calico shirt, and a gun belt holding a heavy revolver. But what shocked Cubby most were the trousers. He couldn't ever remember seeing a woman wearing men's trousers before! These were made of coarse canvas, patched in four or five different places, and rolled up at the cuffs as if she'd bought them too long. Her feet were encased in heavy, scuffed boots, and if it weren't for the very obvious fact that she was a woman, Cubby would never in a million years have guessed it by her outfit.

"What are you doing down here, boy? Spying on me?" she rumbled dangerously, squinting hard at him. He smelled tobacco on her breath, and a faint hint of whiskey there too.

"No—no, I weren't, honest," he croaked.

She studied him. "You been crying, boy?"

He swiped at his eyes and said, "No."

"Don't take to lying unless you can pull it off better than that. Got a name? Course you do. What are you called by?"

My name . . . my name is Cubby."

"Cubby, heh?" She worked her mouth into a knot, turned her face aside and spat a stream of tobacco juice. "If you ain't spying on me, then what are you doing down here?"

"I was—" he didn't know how to say it, and feared she'd quickly see through another lie, and feared what she might do to him if he tried it again. "I was running away," he blurted, and almost instantly wished he had tried out another lie, for now he knew

69

she'd be duty bound to haul him back to his Aunt Doreen."

"Running away. That's why you was crying, heh?" He nodded.

Something changed in her eyes and she considered him a long moment, her mouth working at the chaw inside her cheek. Then in the softest, kindest voice like his ma used to use, she said, "You poor dear. I know how you must be feeling. I run away from home when I was but a tyke myself. You hungry?"

He hadn't eaten since early morning when they all had taken a bit of roasted antelope back on the trail, and he was hungry. But because of all that had happened that day, he had hardly noticed until now that she reminded him.

She spat again and said, "Come along with me, Cubby. I got dinner in the skillet. You can share the campfire with me. Oh, by the by, you can call me Patty."

"Yes, ma'am."

"Now don't go 'ma'aming' me, Cubby. That's for sophisticated women. Just plain Patty will do, I thank you." She turned and climbed the four or five feet to the ledge above and gave Cubby a hand up to the top. Her grip was firm as a man's and her hands rougher than a hard-rock miner's. Not far away sat a tall freight wagon, its tongue stretching out in front of it, propped at the end upon a section of log. Beyond and scattered about were six hobbled mules. There was a bale of hay broken open but the animals seemed to prefer the abundant grass of this place. The town was a few hundred yards to the south and the copper roof of Aunt Doreen's grand house could be seen looming above the treetops.

"This yours?" he asked.

"Yessiree. I've been hauling freight for the U.P. almost since it put down rails," she replied. He wasn't sure, but he thought he detected a distinct note of pride in that.

"I don't usually have company for dinner, Cubby. You just take a sit there on that log by the fire while I wrestle you up a plate and some eatin' ware." Patty disappeared into the back of the empty freight wagon and banged around inside it like she was tossing crates all about, making nearly as much noise as his Uncle Alroy's peddler wagon on a bumpy road. "Here you go," she said, hopping off the back of the freighter and wiping the dust off a tin plate with an old shirt she used for a rag.

Patty busied herself over the fire where an iron grate sat upon a circle of rocks. She had three pans steaming on the grate, two of them covered. A coffeepot perked off to one side where she'd banked up a right handsome bed of glowing coals. Patty was a hand at campfire cooking, like his Uncle Alroy had been. Cubby reckoned the traveling way of life made a person right clever at such skills. He thought of his Aunt Doreen and, try as he might, could not picture her cooking anything over an open campfire.

"Got me some de-lectable victuals here, Cubby. Seared antelope steak in buffalo lard, breaded and seasoned to a right fanciful flavor. Wild onions, and carrots got from the grocer in town and a whole pot full of corn dodgers. Sound good to you?"

Cubby nodded, his mouth beginning to water at the thought of it.

Patty lifted a heavy iron lid and ladled out golden crusty balls from the boiling grease and put them in a ribbed tin to drain. "Hum-hum, looky at them dodgers," she gushed. Then she plucked the tin lid off the skillet and a cloud of steam rose from the hissing steaks there. The odor was wonderful! Cubby fidgeted upon the log and leaned closer.

Patty grinned, proudly displaying the four or five teeth left in her mouth. "Now these here vegetables," she explained, poking them around the third skillet with a wooden fork, are sautéing in gen-u-ine olive oil brung all the way over the ocean on a boat from Italy."

"Really?"

"Really! Here, take a look." She passed a yellow tin can over to him. "You can read, can't you?"

"Some."

"What do you make of that?"

Cubby puzzled over the letters on the can and shook his head. "I can't read it."

"Course you can't! That there is I-talian writing. Proves what I say, don't it."

"Yes, ma'am—er, Patty, I mean."

Patty filled his plate and they sat together eating. It was some of the best food he had ever tasted—certainly superior to any camp food he'd eaten. Even better than what his Uncle Alroy had ever fixed, and Alroy had been a hand at campfire cooking too.

Afterward, scrubbing his mouth with a scrap of cloth that served as a napkin, Cubby was absolutely contented. But then he remembered he was running away and a frown came involuntarily to his face.

Patty collected the dishes, deposited them in a metal washtub and then settled down in the shade of her wagon with a tin cup of coffee.

"Want some?" she asked. "Ain't got no milk nor nothing fancy that a tyke might prefer."

"I drank coffee with my Uncle Alroy," he said.

"Right 'nough, I reckon," and she filled a cup for him. But it was too hot to hold and he set it upon the ground between his feet to let it cool some.

"Now, tell me some about you running away."

"I ain't going back."

She grinned like a jack-o'-lantern. "I wouldn't send you back. You're old 'nough to make your own way in the world."

Though it's what he wanted to hear, for some reason her reply caused a funny hollowness to begin expanding inside his well-filled belly.

"I reckon you have a last name," she said.

"I do. It's Gallagher."

"So, Cubby Gallagher, why are you leaving?"

"Because my Aunt Doreen doesn't want me. Nobody wants me."

"Your Aunt Doreen?" Patty glanced across the way to the roof peeking over the treetops. "You mean *that* Doreen?" she asked, hooking a thumb at the mansion.

Cubby nodded

"Not surprised to hear it," Patty said. "I done a lot of hauling for the U.P., and I knowed Horace Taylor right enough. He was a pusher and a mover, he was. Always figuring out how to turn a profit, and not caring how many toes he stepped on doing so. And I've seen that hoity-toity wife of his a few times, always seemed to be taking in the smell above other folks' heads, if you catch my drift." Patty reared back, burst out with a hoarse laugh and slapped her leg, raising a small cloud of dust from the trousers.

Cubby tried to picture it in his head and decided it must be a grown-up joke.

Suddenly Patty stopped laughing and peered hard at him. "You're related to Doreen Taylor? That means you must be kin to Alroy Gallagher? Are you *that* Gallagher?"

"Alroy was my Uncle."

"Was?"

Cubby's voiced cracked. "He was murdered on the road the other day."

"Murdered?" Suddenly her eyes popped wide. "Was that his wagon burned by them Injuns?"

"It was his wagon bu—"

"Why, the murdering savages," she growled, whipping her big revolver from its holster and shaking it in the air. "If'n I like to lay eyes on 'em that killed Alroy, it's off to that happy hunting grounds they go, and may the heathens learn real quick what sulfur and brimstone smells like!"

"But it weren't Indians," Cubby said.

"Not Injuns? I seen it with my own eyes how they scalped that poor fellow."

"No, it was some bad men that followed us up from Dixon what done it, Patty. They shot Uncle Alroy and burned his wagon, and they'd have done me in for sure too, if my friend, Nan-ta-kee, hadn't been there. He whupped the one coming after me and scalped him just for a warning to the others not to follow."

Patty looked confused. "Haul up there a minute, Cubby. You mean to tell me white men done killed Alroy? And that an Injun saved your hide?"

"That's the way it happened."

Patty returned the revolver to its holster. "That sorta puts a different slant to it, don't it?"

"You knew my Uncle?"

"Oh, sure, Cubby. I've know Alroy for years. From time to time we'd pass each other on the road and stop and have us a good jaw. Or sometimes we'd meet up in a town, him hawking his wares and me dropping off a load of bobwire or cookstoves, or whatever." Patty's voice changed, gentling down some like it had when he'd told her he was running away. "Alroy was a good man." She shook her head, then shot Cubby a quick look. "Not that I'd ever be dumb enough to buy any of his humbug remedies," she added gruffly. "I've a head on my shoulders and I ain't been taken for a sucker since I kicked that scoundrel, Flannigan Bamgardner, out of my life fifteen years ago."

"I don't think he wanted me to live with him either," Cubby said. "If he had, he wouldn't have wanted to take me to live with Aunt Doreen."

Patty frowned. "So you are gonna up and run away?"

He nodded.

"I reckon that's one way to handle the problem. How old are you, Cubby?"

"Ten."

"You have plans?"

"I figured I'd climb aboard a train heading to Cheyenne, then make my way down to Denver. I used to live in Denver. I got friends there."

"I see. Sounds like a good plan to me."

He had been staring at the scuffed toes of his boots, and looked up at that. "You ain't going to make me go back?"

"Already said I wouldn't."

"Oh." That squirming inside his gut began again.

"In fact, I'll help you along your way. Ain't got much I can give you except some advice."

"What advice?"

"I spend a lot of time living out of door like you're gonna be doing, so pay heed to what Patty has to tell you. First, you gotta remember that nighttime comes of a sudden out away from town. The sun goes down and in no time it's so dark you can hardly see your own hand before your eyes. So, soon as you see evening coming, find yourself someplace safe to

75

bed down for the night. If you can find a railroad trestle and crawl up under it real close to them timber bulkheads, you can miss some of the rain and wind. You'll have to get used to sleeping on rocky ground of course, but that comes with practice."

Cubby thought of the featherbed at his aunt's house.

"You're gonna have to wrestle yourself up a blanket too. I'd give you one if I had an extra, but I don't. Nighttime gets mighty cold hereabouts, even in the middle of summer, and we're moving near to fall already. Come another few weeks and you'll be in for brisk sleeping." She gave an indifferent shrug. "When your body takes to shaking like a drunk away from drink, that's just its way of keeping warm. You'll get used to that too." Patty moved the chaw about her cheek as if considering something. "Say, how many fireplaces does that big house over yonder have?"

"I don't know. Didn't have time to count."

"Humph. Bet that mean old aunt of yours don't get cold in her soft bed at night."

"Reckon not," Cubby said, unhappily.

"Now, one more thing. Always collect food where you find it. Don't let nothing slip by you or you'll be hungry all the time. I hear rummaging through the garbage bins behind restaurants and boarding-houses is a good place to find victuals. But watch out for strangers while making your way. Some will steal your food and blanket." She leaned closer, glanced side to side and whispered, "Some will even cut your throat for them things, so keep a sharp eye peeled."

Cubby gulped. He hadn't thought of all that. "What about Indians?" he asked.

"Injuns? Why, they are about. Plenty of 'em.

Crafty they are too. They can sneak up on you with hardly a sound, and before you know it—" Patty dragged a finger across her throat and made a slicing sound through her teeth.

Cubby winced.

Patty stood and made a face in a scrap of a mirror hanging off the side of her wagon. She plucked a long hair from her chin and looked back at him. "Keep them things in mind, Cubby, and chances are probably better than forty–sixty you'll make Denver City." She grinned and went back to examining her chin in the mirror. "Don't worry 'bout them dishes. I'll clean up. You best be on your way if you want to catch the next train east. I think there might be one pulling out in the hour."

Cubby got reluctantly to his feet. Suddenly he was not so eager to leave. Uncertainty kept him rooted there. "Thank you for the food," he said.

"Welcome," she said, making faces at herself.

"Er—will I see you again?" he asked.

"Likely not. I don't much get down to Denver City."

He scraped at the ground with his shoe.

"Well, what are you waiting for?" Patty looked over her shoulder at him. "Denver City is a powerful long piece away from here."

"I . . . I ain't got a blanket," he said.

"You'll find one somewhere."

"Don't have no jacket either."

She squinted at him. "Sounds like you ain't exactly ready to be running away then."

"What should I do?" Suddenly Cubby didn't want to leave. He didn't want to stay either. He didn't know what he wanted.

Patty came back and settled her wide bottom

upon the log that Cubby had been using for a chair. "I'll tell you what I'd do."

"What?" He sat beside the heavy woman.

"I'd be making plans, that's what. Make my plans first, and *then* make my move."

"You mean like finding a blanket and jacket?"

"Don't own one?"

"Everything got burned up."

She spat a brown stream off to one side. "Then maybe your best plan right now is to stay put a while longer. Your aunt will give you a blanket and a jacket just 'cause she's got to. Then when you're ready, then you can hit the rails for Denver town or anywhere else you want to go. That's what I'd do."

Cubby didn't understand it, but suddenly that gnawing in the pit of his stomach let up. "I'll go back and make plans."

"There you go!" Patty grinned and gave him a mighty wallop upon his back that nearly knocked him off the log. "Now you're thinking, Cubby. Now you're planning."

Chapter Seven

Cubby climbed over the iron fence, grabbing the overhanging limb of a cottonwood tree for balance, then jumped down into his Aunt Doreen's backyard. He was making his way toward the fire escape when a voice spoke nearby.

"Hi. Who are you?"

The flushed face of the boy next door was peering at him through two wrought-iron rails. The little dog was there, his black nose poking through, his tail beating faster than the drummer in the Denver City annual Fourth of July parade.

"Hello," Cubby said, his foot poised upon the first step of the fire escape. He glanced up at the window to his room so high above, white curtains fluttering gently in a breeze. He hoped his aunt hadn't discovered his truancy, or that Christine had not returned to finish readying the room for him. "I can't talk. I gotta get back inside."

"I seen you sneak out the window," the boy said.

"I, ah, I was just going out for a walk."

"The Taylors have a front door."

Cubby figured this boy was too nosy for his liking. His face seemed much redder up close, and he looked to be fed real good. His girth was about twice that of Cubby, yet he was no taller. The white-and-black at his side yapped and fanned its tail so fast it gyrated the puppy side to side.

"What's your name?"

"Cubby Gallagher."

"I'm Andy Horvath," the boy announced, taking the pup up into his arms. "And this here is Huck. Want to pet him? You can."

Cubby weighed the options and decided the puppy was more fun than sitting alone in that sissified room. "All right."

Huck was ecstatic at the attention. Andy laughed, then set the dog down and sat upon the ground. Cubby kneeled on the other side of the fence and gave Huck a good hard scratching.

"Why did you name him Huck?"

" 'Cause he was a runaway, least that's what my ma and pa figured. And someday Huck and me, we are gonna have us some great adventures. Once he gets a little bigger we're going to the Indian Cave."

"What's that?"

"A cave, about a mile from here. My pa took me to see it once. Indians used to live there and we found arrowheads and bones and other great things."

"Wow."

"Where did you come from?" Andy asked, turning Huck over upon his lap and giving him a belly rub."

"Denver City. I grew up there."

"How old are you?"

"Ten."

"So am I. You gonna stay long?"

Cubby didn't have an answer to that. According to what he had overheard, it didn't sound as if he would be there long. "I don't know. My ma and pa died, and my Uncle Alroy got killed. I'm suppose to live with my Aunt Doreen now, but I don't know how long that is gonna last."

"Mrs. Taylor is your aunt?" Andy's eyes widened. They were a sort of green color, with gold flecks in them.

"Yes."

Andy pretended to shiver. "You're gonna live in that big house?"

"For a while, I reckon."

Andy looked around, then lowered his voice. "You better be careful then."

"Why?"

"Because that place is haunted."

"Haunted?"

"There's a ghost that comes out almost every night. I seen it myself."

"No. Really?"

"Yes. My bedroom is right there," he pointed to the nearest window of a low gray house that stood a couple dozen feet away, half hidden behind a row of lilac bushes. "Sometimes when it's late at night and I can't sleep, I put my lamp out and sit there by that window, watching. And that's when I see her."

"Who?"

"The ghost."

Cubby gulped. "A real ghost?"

"Sure enough. It's a woman dressed all in a flowing white veil. She appears late at night and moves around the yard, like a bit of smoke. And sometimes

81

I hear her moan, and sometimes I see other ghosts with her too."

Cubby glanced at the yard. In the daylight it looked plain as any other yard he'd ever seen. Just the same, a small shiver crawled up his spine.

"I think she's an Indian maiden. Sure enough I bet you that house is built atop an old Indian burial ground," Andy said in a low voice, his green eyes shifting past Cubby. "I seen an Indian once, standing behind the fence looking in. Me and Huck, we chased him off." Andy puffed up some and bragged, "I'm not at all a-feared of Indians. I'll bet that Indian knew he had kin buried there. That's why he was staring over the fence."

"Maybe that's why Aunt Doreen has so many gophers," Cubby suggested, but Andy wasn't paying attention.

"Me and Jack Wingate, we seen a whole tribe of Indians once. They was Sioux, and they was traveling in a pack, taking all their stuff up north somewhere. We followed them to their camp. I wanted to sneak on down and steal a bow and some arrows, but Jack was too a-scared to. You ever have any adventures, Cubby?"

Cubby had led a pretty plain life up until recently, and the way Andy had asked the question, he reckoned that whatever he came up with, the red-faced boy would manage to better him with an adventure of his own. But Cubby figured he did have something that Andy couldn't top, not in a hundred years.

"I run with Indians myself," he started, hoping to make it sound as if it were a little thing, as if this were something that happened every day to him. "My Indian name is War Hatchet. I got a friend named Nan-ta-kee. He's Apache."

"You got an Apache for a friend?"

"Sure." He said it easy-like, as if it were most natural and normal to hang around with Apaches.

"We went off killing and scalping once," Cubby said, yanking out a blade of grass and sticking it nonchalantly into the corner of his mouth. "Yep, we took a white man's scalp, and then we stole his horse," he continued, adding a little bit of salt to spice the story up some.

Andy stared a moment, then said, "Yeah? Think I was born yesterday? Where is your Apache friend?"

"Oh, he's around," Cubby said casually, enjoying the suspicion in Andy's young face.

"You don't know no Indian," Andy said.

"Do too."

"Do not."

Cubby stood. "I do too know an Apache. Now I got to go before they find I'm gone."

"You mean you snuck out?" Andy's voice held a note of excitement.

"I did. I was figuring to run away, but changed my mind." Cubby started back to the long flight of switchbacking stairs.

"You were really going to run away?"

"Might still do so."

"Hey, Cubby."

"What?"

"You want to do something later?"

"Maybe." Cubby wasn't sure he liked Andy Horvath. He didn't take to braggarts, and that he had been forced to do some bragging of his own to bolster himself in the red-faced boy's eyes irked him now.

"We can look for ghosts tonight. I sometimes sneak out too. I'll come get you later."

"Well . . ." There was something intriguing about looking for ghosts. And if Aunt Doreen's house really was haunted, Cubby wasn't sure he wanted to be alone. "All right. I'll see you later." He hurried up the stairs and slipped unseen back into his room and shut the window.

Nantaje and Keane rode back into town and after some searching Nantaje pointed and said, "There is his horse." He and Keane reined their animals across the street and hitched them to the rail in front of a general mercantile store. Inside, Lionel was paying the clerk for a pile of supplies stacked on the counter. The shopkeeper looked up at the jangling of the bell and stared at Nantaje. The Apache was used to such reaction and ignored the man. He could hardly blame him. An Indian dressed in faded army blues was not exactly an everyday sight in these parts. Down Tombstone way where Nantaje had spent the last half dozen years scouting for General Crook, such sights were common place.

"We wondered where you got off to," Keane said. "Stocking up?" He nodded at the pile.

"I'm leaving," Lionel said, gathering the supplies into his arms.

"Still heading for California?"

"Dat ain't changed. Only de company has." Lionel walked out the door and began filling his saddle-bags.

Keane leaned against the railing and said, "Don't let Louvel get under your skin. He sometimes has a grating way about him, but that's just the way he is. He didn't mean anything."

"I know his kind. Got de scars on my back to prove it. I run away from his kind years ago, when I wasn't too much older than Cubby am."

"And you're still running," Keane said.

Lionel glared at him. "What do yo' know about anything?"

"I know we are all running away from something, Lionel. Nantaje, Ridere, O'Brian, you, me. And I think of us all, Louvel is running the hardest. He's running away from the here and now, trying to find a past that no longer exists."

"No reason he should think himself better than de rest of us."

"I agree with you there, Lionel. But like I said, Louvel has a way of grating on you, if you let him."

"He thinks he am gonna find his past with dat woman?"

"I don't know what he thinks, but there is no denying Mrs. Taylor *is* someone from his past."

"She am no good for him."

"Who's to say, Lionel? But in matters of the heart, a wise man keeps his opinions to himself."

Lionel frowned and his anger cooled. "Maybe I opened my mouth when I should have kept it shut." He looked at the two of them and said, "Where is he, anyway?"

"Louvel took off right after you did. Seems I should have kept my mouth shut too. But I suspect he didn't get much farther than the closest barber and bathhouse."

"One thing is sure," Nantaje put in, "Louvel is not leaving town right away."

Keane frowned. "No, he's not. I'm thinking maybe we ought to hang around a day or two to see how this plays itself out."

"I thought you might, John Russell. Want me to take the horse to the livery?"

Keane nodded and handed his reins to the Apache. "I'll see if I can't round up O'Brian and Ridere, then find us some rooms at the hotel." Keane paused, turning back to Lionel. "You staying or riding?"

A small twitch of indecision puckered the corner of Lionel's lips, then he nodded. "I'll stay."

"Good."

"I better go with Mr. Nantaje and help him see dat these horses am put up proper."

"There he is," Cooper Brawley said, turning away from the window. They were in the Bitter-Sweet Saloon, at a table with a view of the main street. Brawley had just rocked back on his chair to check again and now the chair thumped down on all fours.

Burl Rahn was fingering a glass of whiskey, not drinking much. He wasn't in the mood, not with last night's hangover still lingering. So much had gone wrong since that night three nights earlier in Dixon when they had trifled with that peddler, and had been suckered into using the cream that had made most of their hair fall out. No one had intended to kill him. It had just happened. Then Kersten got himself scalped. Rahn wondered what else was going to go wrong.

"Is that big man with him? Them two are always hanging together."

"No, he went another way. It's that colored fellow with him this time, Burl," Brawley said. "Looks like the two of them are taking the horses down to the livery."

"Let me see." Rahn peered out the window, then motioned his partners to the door. They followed the Apache and black man to the end of town and watched them take the horses inside the big barn there. Once the two men were out of sight, Rahn, Brawley and Langston crossed the street and moved among a row of dilapidated sheds that had been thrown up by the railroad some years back and then abandoned. They worked their way to the back of the stable and Rahn pressed his face to a dingy window there. But all he could see were a row of horse stalls.

"Shouldn't we wait until it's dark?" Langston wondered, craning his neck to see if anyone had taken notice of their suspicious scurrying from building to building.

"I want to see where they go from here," Rahn said, moving to the corner of the building to wait. When the Indian and black man emerged from the livery and started back into town, Rahn said, "Somehow we got to cut that Injun from that herd he runs with."

"He sticks close, all right," Langston agreed.

"Come on, let's see where they're headed." They moved out, trying to look casual and keeping back so as not to attract attention.

"What about the kid?" Brawley asked in a low voice as they made their way toward the center of town.

"He shouldn't be no trouble. We'll just keep an eye on that house and grab him when he comes out alone. I'll cut his throat before he has a chance to cry out."

Langston winced and glanced away.

"No time to go soft on me, Kleef," Rahn said, catching the look. "That kid knows enough to put a rope around all our necks."

Up ahead the Indian and the black man met a man coming out of the hotel Rahn remembered seeing earlier. They spoke a moment, then all headed toward a saloon across the way. Rahn and his buddies went back to the saloon and Rahn peered over the batwing doors into the darkened, smoke-filled room. He spied the Indian at a table with four other men. The one-armed man he had seen earlier wasn't among them.

They moved down the street a way and turned down an alley to talk.

"The way I count it, there is five, maybe six men hanging together."

Langston rolled himself a cigarette and passed the pouch around. "That can make for a tough cut," he said, putting a match to his smoke. "It might be we're going to have to fight our way through two or three of them just to get to that Injun. And if so, I want no part of it. I'll take my chances that nothing will ever come of that peddler's killing."

"Maybe you'll take your chances, but I won't," Rahn said.

"Might be we are heaping more trouble on us going after him. Kleef could be right. We let it drop here and now, nothing will come of it."

"There is no backing out, not now," Rahn said. "If we do we will always be looking over our shoulders. That Injun will go off on his own, if only to take care of nature. And when he does, we'll be waiting for him."

"And in the meantime while we are hanging around here waiting for the redskin to take a leak, the boss will be giving our jobs away," Langston reminded him.

"I can always get another job," Rahn shot back. "But I only got one neck, and I don't aim to hand it over to the hangman."

Brawley said, "I'm inclined to agree with Kleef. We might be making more trouble for ourselves not letting it alone. I'll give it another day, Burl. If we can't do it by then I'm heading back."

Rahn bristled at this challenge to his authority but

he restrained himself. He was facing a mutiny and one wrong word now might send Langston and Brawley over the sides of the jolly boat.

"We'll have it done by tomorrow," Rahn said confidently.

That quelled the uprising, at least for the moment, and they went back to the Bitter-Sweet Saloon to wait and keep an eye out for the Indian.

Chapter Eight

Royden Louvel grabbed an overhead bar with his one hand, heaved himself from the tub of once warm water, now practically cool to the touch. Stepping out of the tub, he grinned at the gray scum across the water. "More trail dust than on the rear end of a stampeding buffalo," he noted to himself, reaching for the towel. He dried himself inside the small canvas-sided cubicle, then stepped out into the room where three other similar enclosures were. He could hear gruff singing coming from a stall to his left. The other two were unoccupied this late in the day.

Louvel peered into a steamed mirror and dragged his hand against the grain of the whiskers that rounded his chin and upper lip, following the hollows of his gaunt cheeks. He frowned at the dusty clothes he'd shed, lying in a heap upon a wooden bench, and was loath to crawl back inside them. It was either that or go on naked through the door for his shave. Snapping his shirt and trousers and raising a cloud of dust, he dressed and stepped through the hanging cloth that served as a door and down a short hallway. The barber was waiting for him. Louvel settled himself into the chair and closed his eyes contentedly as the man buried his face beneath warm, fragrant lather.

Sitting there, eyes closed, feeling the razor skimming his cheeks, Louvel thought of Doireann Taylor. It was curious and amusing, but each time he tried to remember exactly how she looked, the face that swam before his closed eyelids belonged to a girl, not the woman she had become. Try as he might, the face always changed to that of a sixteen-year-old girl, right down to the laughing voice. Louvel grinned and was warned by the barber that he was liable to lose a part of his lip if he did that again.

The door opened, and the heavy steps of a man come through.

"Be with you in a few minutes," the barber said. A chair creaked, followed by the rustle of a newspaper being opened.

Louvel spent the next few minutes reliving those days long ago, before the war. Those pleasant days under the old rule when a man's heritage and the old traditions of the land still meant something to men—men willing to die for them!

Then the barber was toweling off his face and splashing scented toilet water onto his cheeks. "There you go, mister. That will be forty cents for the bath and shave."

Louvel paid the man and started to leave.

"You smell pretty enough to kiss." Keane's voice came from behind the newspaper. He folded it aside and said, "I hope Mrs. Taylor appreciates the effort."

"Major Keane. What are you doing here?"

Keane got to his feet and pulled at his chin. "Figured I needed a shave too." He grinned.

"Uh-huh," Louvel muttered suspiciously.

Keane's bulk filled the barber's chair and he leaned back. The barber wrapped his face in a hot towel. "Where are you headed now, Captain?"

"Ah have a few items to tend to before my engagement tonight, suh," the southerner replied stiffly. Louvel knew it wasn't by chance Keane was here. "Was there something you wished to say to me, Major?"

"Yes, there was, but doing so through a pile of hot towels is inconvenient. I found the local newspaper entertaining."

Louvel got his point. Keane had something on his mind, something he wanted to keep private. "Ah will peruse it as you are finishing your shave," he said.

"I found the article about an ongoing investigation into the loss of some railroad funds curious."

Louvel took a seat and absently leafed through the pages. There were only four of them, but nothing in particular caught his attention. His thoughts kept straying back to Doireann Taylor. She seemed to go by the name Doreen these days. He recalled that was how Charles had addressed her. Back in the old days Charles always called her "Miss Doireann," like everyone else. Well, what did he expect? She's no longer a sixteen-year-old girl. She was a woman, a well-to-do woman at that. Doreen fit her better these days, Louvel decided.

Then suddenly Keane was standing over him and Louvel was surprised the time had passed so quickly. "Reckon I'm about as pretty as you now," Keane joked.

"That will be the day," Louvel retorted.

Keane laughed. "Well, one thing is for sure, we both smell better."

Outside, Louvel removed a bundle from his saddle. "Ah was told there is a tailor who would brush and sponge my suit."

"You going to wear that?"

"Ah feel it will be appropriate," Louvel said.

"At the very least it will raise some eyebrows."

"Then so be it."

They started down the boardwalk. "There was something you wanted to say to me, Major?"

"Yes, there was. Earlier on the street, you rode off before you let me finish what I was saying."

"If you have come to chide me further on the matter of my attitude, suh, let me tell you right now Ah'm not interested in hearing it."

"No, I haven't come to do that, Louvel."

"Then what?"

"I just wanted to say that if I spoke of matters that were none of my business, I wanted to apologize."

"Apologize?" Louvel stopped and looked at the man who towered a full head over him and was nearly wide as a door frame. There was that easy smile, with not the least bit of consternation at coming to him this way. It would not have been easy for Louvel to have done the same. In spite of himself there was much about this big northerner that he admired, although he would never admit that to anyone. Louvel managed a grin and shook his head. "For a damned Yankee, you certainly have your ways, Major Keane."

"I like to keep morale up among the troops," Keane said. They had started walking again.

"There you go again, forgetting you are no longer in the army."

"You know what they say about old habits."

93

"Hum. So Ah have heard."

"Lionel realizes he spoke out of turn too."

Louvel stiffened at that, but before he could frame a response they arrived at the tailor shop. A short man in striped trousers and a white shirt took the bundle from Louvel. He said he would see to it while they waited, and carried the bundle into a back room, where the sound of steam and the odor of moist wool drifted from the doorway.

Some twenty minutes later the short man re-emerged from the steaming back room, Louvel's clothes brushed and pressed, the stains expertly sponged off of them. The man wore a curious look as he handed the clothes to Louvel. "What are you going to do with these?"

"Wear them," Louvel answered sharply.

"Oh," the man replied briefly, backing down from the challenging tone in Louvel's voice.

Louvel paid the man and went back to the hotel with Keane. After Louvel had changed into the clothes, he asked Keane to help him fasten the red sash about his waist, for it was difficult to do one-armed. Upon the cuff of the empty right sleeve, a fine gold braid had been sewn. Louvel fastened it over one of the coat's breast buttons and turned to regard himself in the mirror. The reflection of the Confederate uniform caused a bit of moisture to gather in his eyes.

"I'll say it again, Louvel, you look spiffy enough to shoot."

"And I will repeat, you damned Yankees tried mighty hard to do it."

Keane laughed. "You'll want an escort, perhaps. Just in case someone decides they don't like the color of your outfit?"

"No, suh, this is one ride Ah wish to make alone."

It was almost time. Louvel and Keane went downstairs and through the lobby. Louvel turned plenty of heads as he strode boldly to his horse and stepped up into the saddle.

The afternoon was late and dusk was coming on. Across the street, Ridere, O'Brian, Lionel and Nantaje stepped out of the saloon as Louvel turned his horse from the rail and rode away. Nantaje crossed the rutted road and joined Keane on the other side.

"There goes one stubborn, single-minded, bull-headed hombre," Keane said.

"You two are much alike."

Keane looked surprised. "How so?"

"Your feelings run deep and hot, like the blood of a warrior."

Keane would have denied it, except he knew that Nantaje was right.

"John Russell. Look there." The Apache pointed. On the street corner stood the man they had seen earlier with the newspaper. He was watching Louvel ride toward that big house at the edge of town.

"They are multiplying," Keane said, noting a second man with him now. The two were dressed nearly the same; both looking like pugilists in their tight jackets and bowler hats.

"Like rabbits," Nantaje said.

"Or rats." Keane made a face as if he'd suddenly discovered a foul odor.

The men made no attempt to hide their curiosity. Speaking suddenly with their heads close together, one nodded and started down toward the livery and the railroad yards beyond. The other tucked his folded newspaper under his arm and strode up Commerce Street at a brisk pace.

"What do you make of that?" Keane asked.

Nantaje said, "You want me to follow him?"

Keane considered a moment. "It wouldn't hurt to see what those two are up to. You take the one heading for the livery. I'll keep an eye on the yahoo ghosting Louvel."

"Right."

"Nantaje."

The Apache stopped and looked back at him.

"Try to keep out of trouble. Be inconspicuous."

Nantaje grinned. "Don't worry about me, John Russell. I have had a lot of practice staying out of the white man's way."

Try as he might to be inconspicuous, in a town full of white men, Nantaje stood out like an apple in a basket full of bananas. Everyone was curious, but no one dared come too close, giving him a wide berth on the sidewalk. Ahead, the man in the suit strode purposefully toward the edge of town where lay the rail yards and huge freight buildings. Now he stopped and glanced left to right.

Nantaje stopped too and backed into an alleyway so as not to be seen. He could clearly see the face now; the sunburned skin and the nose that had been broken a time or two. There was a bulge in his coat beneath his left arm. The man waited for a couple of freight wagons to rumble past, heading for the warehouses, then crossed the street, hurrying now through the weeds growing between the rows of siding tracks.

Railroad cars stood about everywhere, and here and there were ramshackle buildings, every one surrounded with cluttering cast-offs of the railroad business and looking like they were only waiting for a good wind to turn them into a heap of scrap lumber.

Being careful not to get too close, Nantaje lost

sight of the man for a moment. This type of trailing was foreign to the Apache, accustomed to the vast open deserts of southern Arizona. A cluttered freight yard threw up challenges he had not faced before. The nearest he could liken it to was trailing a man through rocky country, like some areas of the Dragoon Mountains.

He picked him up again and scurried along a row of empty cattle cars to keep him in sight. But he lost him again beyond a solid-sided freight car. Nantaje rushed recklessly between two cars, hunching low to the ground, and darted across a strip of weeds. But when he had gotten around the car, the man was gone. He'd simply disappeared among rows of empty railroad cars. Nantaje waited, not moving, eyes and ears searching for a trace. But the man was gone.

The Apache was vaguely perplexed at how he could have lost the white man so easily. Then he understood. The man had slipped inside one of these many cars. Did he know he was being followed? Nantaje didn't think so, and he was determined to search for his prints among the weeds and see exactly when he had disappeared, when all at once a sound reached him from another direction. People were moving through the weeds. A stick snapped softly, cinders crunched underfoot.

Nantaje dropped behind a rusty wheel and peered beneath the belly of a freight car. For a moment nothing moved, then down by one of the weathered shacks, Nantaje saw a man moving cautiously along the wall. Then a second one appeared and they stopped, putting their heads together. A third fellow suddenly slipped from the gathering shadows on the other side of the shack.

Nantaje didn't move, squinting into the growing

dusk. There was something about these men . . . then his eyes widened with surprise. These were the same three he had spied back on the trail, the three who had murdered War Hatchet's uncle and burned his wagon. The same ones, Nantaje realized, as anger turned his blood hot, who had tried to murder War Hatchet!

They started forward again, fanning out and drawing their guns as they moved stealthily through the yard. Nantaje's hand reached for his knife, then stopped. A scowl crossed his usually impassive face. This was not the time or place for revenge. The white man's town was dangerous enough for an Indian; if someone were to witness him making short work of these three murderers, he had no doubt it would mean a quick trip to the gallows—if he even made it that far.

They were close now. Nantaje grabbed the iron rungs that climbed the side of the car and scrambled up them, flattening himself upon the roof. He lost sight of them, but his ears told him they had drawn near and were easing through the weeds where a few moments before he had lain in hiding.

"You sure he went this way, Burl?" The voice spoke softly.

"Kleef seen that Injun come this way," Burl growled impatiently.

"It's getting dark and I don't like this. You saw what he done to Lars."

"Worried about losing more of that hair?" Burl said, scorn in his voice. "Between the two of us we ain't got enough left worth taking, thanks to that peddler."

Footsteps approached from the left, and then a whispered voice said, "He's not back there."

"Then he's got to be ahead," Burl replied.

"We're just wasting our time trying to get to the buck," one of them said. "It's that kid we need to be worrying about, not the Injun. Even if that Injun did see us, he ain't going to the law."

"Maybe you're right," Burl said. "Anyway, he went and scalped Lars, didn't he? That makes him about as guilty as us. All right, we'll let the Injun go. We're running out of time anyway. Let's go take care of that kid."

Their footsteps faded in the distance. Nantaje slipped over the side of the car and climbed down to the ground. It was almost dark and the man he'd been following was long gone. He went back into town, keeping an eye out for the three murderers, and met Keane coming down Commerce Street.

"The yahoo is just standing there on the corner right where we saw him the first time. He takes a walk around the block from time to time, but that's about all."

"I lost my man in the rail yard, John Russell."

"Too bad. Well, it's probably not important. I suppose we ought to see what the others are up to."

"My guess is, they are getting drunk somewhere."

Keane grinned. "Ridere and O'Brian at least, and Lionel's probably with them too." He started across the street, but stopped when Nantaje didn't move. "Coming?"

"No, I think I will take a look around town, John Russell."

"All right. But remember—"

"I know. Stay out of trouble."

Keane frowned suddenly. "What is it you got in mind?"

Nantaje was about to tell Keane what he had heard, but decided against it. This was becoming a personal matter, and Nantaje was of a mind to handle such things by himself. "You know me, John Russell. I need to be out there where the wind and the coyotes live. Too many people around make me nervous."

Keane let it drop, but as Nantaje strode away toward the end of town, he knew the tall ex-army major hadn't completely bought the story. John Russell knew him too well for that.

Chapter Nine

"Royden," Doreen said, catching her breath and staring at him standing in her doorway. Maybe she was seeing a ghost from out of her past. He couldn't tell if she was pleased or not. He wanted to please Doreen Taylor—that was all he had ever wanted, when this striking woman wore pigtails and went by the name Doireann. She *was* seeing a ghost; the specter of their shared past; a fleeting shadow of what had once been the living pulse and breath of the South. Her view moved down the gray jacket and lingered a moment upon the empty sleeve.

"You look gallant, Royden."

"Ah was hoping you would appreciate it," he replied, peering down at the gray uniform with the scarlet sash. It was threadbare and mended in half a dozen places; lovingly cared for all these years, for Louvel fully expected to wear it again in the service of his country. But that hope was quickly tarnishing, and though he would never admit it aloud, inside him a pang pricked his heart. Perhaps the South would never rise again?

"Don't just stand there," Doreen said, taking his arm and guiding him through the foyer into the living room. His spirit swelled at the sight of the furniture, and the paintings on the walls. The long staircase that soared overhead caught his eyes and held them a long time, but he wasn't really seeing the staircase. He'd caught a glimpse of his past, a past that Doreen Taylor had managed to capture in its essence in this grand home so very far from their roots in New Orleans. Charles took his hat and they went into a parlor and sat together sipping tea, catching each other up on nearly twenty-five years of history.

When she asked him what he'd been doing all these years, Louvel was embarrassed to admit that he'd been mostly drifting, earning his keep with a deck of cards and his wit.

She told how after the war she had searched for him, but upon word of his death how circumstances had forced her to move north to live with her sister and relatives. "Charles remained at my side, faithful as ever before the war."

Louvel was uncomfortable hearing about her life with Horace Taylor, but he wanted to know it, had to know it all.

"Horace did well for you." Louvel's eyes traversed the papered walls above walnut wainscoting. "Italian?"

"We had it imported."

Paintings in heavy, carved frames graced the walls. The house was filled with polished tables and upholstered chairs. The settee upon which they were sitting had carved arms and feet, and was covered in tapestry.

"Yes. Horace worked hard and made a few good investments," she replied distractedly.

"Did you ever have children?" Louvel ask.

"Children?" Doreen laughed lightly and shook her head. "Goodness gracious no. All the mess, the noise. No thank you, Royden, they just get in the way. I can do very well without the nuisance."

Louvel had always thought it would have been rewarding to rear children, but he conceded her point. Certainly at his age, he'd not want to begin a family . . . but there had been a time. . . .

"And you, Royden?"

He shook his head. "Ah have never married."

"I am surprised. You were something of a prize catch when you were younger. You turned the eyes of all the young ladies. I was jealous of every girl you even looked at. So handsome, so very full of self-confidence . . . so many plans."

"The war changed all of that," he replied. A note of sadness had escaped with his words and now he paused, thinking, and realized he was frowning. Then he smiled at her. "You needn't have been jealous, Doireann. Ah had eyes for only one young lady."

She put a hand upon his. "It is Doreen these days. That other name holds too many unpleasant memories."

"Ah apologize."

Charles came softly into the room and cleared his throat. Doreen turned to him after a moment. "Yes, Charles? What is it?" she said impatiently.

"Dinner is on the sideboard, Miss Doreen, if you and Mr. Louvel are ready."

"Ah am famished," Louvel said, standing.

They followed Charles into the dining room, passing a tall mirror upon the wall, where Doreen slowed to touch her hair in place and smooth the silky material of her yellow dress. The long table was set for two. Charles seated Doreen at the head, and Louvel to her right. Charles and Christine served them off of silver trays, but the dishes appeared old, and some were chipped about the rim. Charles kept the crystal goblets full of a very good white wine.

Afterward, with the dishes cleared away, Doreen raised an eyebrow at Charles and the black servant hurried off. He returned a moment later holding a large wooden humidor, lifted the lid and held the box out to Louvel.

"I know this isn't quite the same as gathering in the gentlemen's parlor with your friends after dinner for whiskey and cigars, but it is all I can offer these days."

Louvel took one of the cigars and passed it slowly beneath his nose, relishing the fragrance and grinning. "It has been years since Ah have had a decent cigar. Cuban?"

"Horace used to have them shipped in from Havana. Those arrived for him only last week." Her voice faltered a bit. "Apparently the manufacturer sent them as a gift, not realizing that poor Horace has been dead for over a year."

Charles clipped the end for him and held the match. Then he brought brandy on a tray.

"I have whiskey if you prefer?"

"This will do fine, thank you," he said.

Swirling the amber liquid in its belled snifter, Louvel followed Doreen into the parlor again. As they sat down Louvel looked about and asked, "Where is Cubby? Ah have not seen him around."

"Master Gallagher is in his room," Doreen replied

sternly, her eyebrows knitting together. "It keeps him from under foot. I haven't quite decided what I am to do with him."

"To do?"

"Well, he certainly can not stay here, can he?"

"Hum. Ah just assumed since he is family—"

"My sister's son," she replied quickly, her voice turning icy. "Elise married down, you know. Married a common laborer. I warned her she'd never amount to anything if she wasn't careful. And I was right. Her husband clerked a store, and his brother was a common peddler, a vagabond who kept flitting from place to place."

Louvel winced, and tried to cover it over. Doreen caught it and added quickly, "But you had a reason for your wanderings, dear Royden. You were lost and seeking." Her voice softened. "But you need seek no further."

"Yes, I feel it is so," Louvel replied, "now that I have found you again."

There was a knock on his door, but before Cubby could reply to it, the door swung open and Christine poked her head inside. "If you are hungry you can eat down in the kitchen with Charles and me."

Cubby followed her out into the hall, but instead of taking the stairs down into the house, she turned to the right, bustling ahead of him to a door standing open. A narrow staircase switched steeply back and forth, passing three closed doors along the way until it reached another standing open. It was the kitchen, and what a kitchen! Cubby figured a body could cook enough food here to feed the whole church back home in Denver City. There was a huge stove, and copper pots and pans on the wall. A worktable stood in the middle of the floor, and a butcher block nearby. Charles, in shirtsleeves, was already seated at a little table, his black jacket hanging over the back of his chair.

"Sit down, Master Cubby," Charles invited with a smile, waving him over. "Bet you am hungry?"

"Not very," Cubby replied, and stopped short of telling him about his aborted runaway attempt, and the wonderful food Patty had served him.

"I know'd how it can be when so much happens of a sudden. Lose your appetite, did you?"

"Yes, sir."

Christine slid a plate before him. Pork chops, boiled potatoes, steamed carrots and broccoli. And there was a pie sitting on the counter where Cubby could watch it as he ate. One thing was certain, if by some miracle he did end up staying here, he'd not want for food. But warmth? That was another thing. Christine was as cool as his Aunt Doreen. Only Charles seemed pleased that he had come to live with them.

Charles said to Cubby, "Miss Doreen wants me to take you into town tomorrow and fit you out with some new clothes. How does that sound?"

"I lost everything when they burned my uncle's wagon."

"Well, we'll fix that right up, Master Cubby."

Cubby liked Charles. The old man always had a smile and a kind word.

"Getting on toward night," Charles noted, glancing at the window, then at Christine. "I best put the carriage away and take the horses over to the livery."

Christine nodded, her mouth full of potatoes.

Cubby said, "Do the gophers come out at night?"

"Gophers?" Charles canted an eye at him. "What gophers?"

"Why, the ones digging all those holes in Aunt Doreen's yard."

Charles went suddenly motionless and gave Christine a quick look. Christine had stopped moving too, her fork frozen in midair, a few inches from her open mouth. But Charles recovered in an instant and then he laughed. "Oh, those gophers. I suspect those critters are all over the place come the witching hour. But I never am up that late to take a good notice, no sir. I am sleeping like a babe." He laughed again and went to furiously shoving his food around his plate.

After dinner Christine told Cubby to return to his room and stopped him when he had started out into the house. "Use the back stairs," she said. "Madam has company."

"It's Captain Louvel, ain't it?"

"Isn't it," she corrected, staring down her long nose at him. "And Madam's business is none of yours."

"But I just want to say hi."

Christine stretched a finger toward the back staircase.

"Yes, ma'am." Cubby's head dropped and he scuffed up the long staircase. He emerged in the hallway even though the stairs continued upward another flight; to the attic, he suspected, thinking that one of these days he would have to explore it.

He closed the door to his room and sat in a chair by the window. It was nearly dark and from this place he could see lights coming on through the treetops where Andy lived. There was a lamp in his room but Cubby didn't light it, preferring to sit in the dark and watch the stars come out and the moon, a mere sliver tonight, rise above the trees. He wondered briefly what time the ghost came out, but he suspected it was just some more of Andy's boastings.

Sitting there all alone, Cubby's thoughts turned back to his Uncle Alroy and he shivered at the memory of how he was murdered. He thought of his parents too, wiping his eyes, trying not to let it get to him like it always did. Then Aunt Doreen's stern face swam into view and Cubby remembered he had plans to make, just like Patty had told him. He'd make his plans and be long gone before his aunt could ship him off to any old orphanage. Thinking about Patty lifted his spirits some.

He was startled by a knock on the door. Again Christine came in without waiting for his okay. "Land of mercy, don't you know how to light a lamp?" she declared.

"I was looking at the stars."

"Stargazing is for lovers and old men, and you ain't neither."

"Aren't either."

Christine's scowl deepened in the light from the hallway. She set something down on the table, fumbled in the dark and struck a match. Her narrow, pinched face showed in the flare of light as she lit the lamp. As the soft glow expanded through the room Cubby saw what it was she had brought.

She filled the china pitcher with hot water from a steaming copper kettle. "Here is soap and towels." She shoved the pile into his hands. "And you'll find a chamber pot under the bed if you need to use it. If you do, make certain you take it out to the privy first thing in the morning, hear? That's not part of my duties."

"Yes, ma'am." Past the open door Cubby could hear voices coming from far below. "Is Captain Louvel still here?"

"He is, and it is none of your business." Christine started for the door.

Cubby frowned. "Ma'am?"

She stopped and scowled back at him.

"Good night, ma'am."

It looked like she might choke on the words, but she said just the same, "Good night, Master Darby." The door closed and he was alone again.

He turned the lamp way down and went back to the chair, staring at his faint reflection in the window glass. He must have fallen asleep, for the next thing he knew, a face was staring back at him . . . and it wasn't his own. He leaped from the chair, then realized it was only Andy Horvath.

Andy had been softly tapping on the window. Now he grinned, amused at Cubby's fright. Cubby snorted impatiently at him and lifted the sash.

"Got you that time," Andy hooted.

"Keep your voice down."

Andy slipped into the room and looked around. Cubby was grateful he couldn't see much in the low light. He wouldn't want Andy to think him a sissy. "What time is it?"

"About ten-thirty."

"What are you doing here?" Then Cubby remembered. "Seen the ghost yet?"

"Nope. We can go into my yard and wait. Got a grand view from the porch roof."

"Just a minute." Cubby went to the door and pulled it open a crack. All the lights were extinguished, except for a faint flicker from somewhere below. He listened. The slow, even tick-tock of a grandfather's clock in the foyer was the only noise in the house. Captain Louvel had left and apparently everyone else had gone to bed.

"Okay," Cubby whispered, closing the door.

109

It was cool out on the fire escape. Cubby wished he owned a jacket, and he suddenly had a keener appreciation of Patty's wisdom. He would have to talk Charles into buying one for him tomorrow if he was ever to do his running away properly. They crept down the stairs, the iron treads ringing lightly beneath their feet, the whole apparatus groaning from time to time and swaying slightly. Cubby hadn't noticed that earlier. The night seemed to have heightened his senses.

Once upon the ground, Andy backed against the ironwork and looked around. He was standing right in the middle of the wilting flower garden and Cubby pulled him off of it.

Andy only grinned. "Gosh, old lady Taylor don't care about these flowers no more," he whispered. "This was something her husband tended to. After he died, it all just went to seed. She never hoes or waters or weeds, or anything anymore."

Just the same, Cubby had a natural aversion to tramping through someone else's flower beds whether they were tended or not. The two boys hurried to the iron fence and scrambled over it, falling behind some shrubs just in case someone was watching. But no one came out to yell at them and Andy led the way to his porch. They climbed a young elm and scrambled onto the porch. It was roofed in tin and Andy tiptoed to the end and sat upon the cold metal.

Cubby saw what Andy had meant. From here they had a perfect view of his Aunt's backyard, the tool shed in the corner, the huge, overarching elm tree near the house, the carriage house and the privy at the back of the lot, the gazebo. Beyond his Aunt's property the dark stand of cottonwood trees marched thickly along the little creek. He strained hard into them, but try as he might, he could not see Patty's campsite, which could not have been too far off. It was plain Patty was asleep too, as Cubby figured he ought to be. He shivered in the cool night air, and hid it from the boy next to him. Andy was in shirtsleeves too, and if he wasn't bothered by the chill, Cubby was determined he wasn't going to be either.

"We'll just wait," Andy whispered excitedly.

Cubby drew up his knees and hugged them to his chest. Peering into the night, he half wanted to see a ghost, and he half wanted not to. Ghosts weren't something to trifle with, and certainly not welcomed guests in a house he was staying in. If his Aunt's house really was haunted, it would be only one more reason to run away.

Something moved behind the wrought-iron fence and a pair of eyes shined back at him. Cubby let go of his breath. It was only a fox. Nearby an owl hooted, sounding spooky.

Cubby shivered again. His view roamed the dark yard and climbed the huge elm at its far end. The tree's branches spread over almost a quarter of the property, reaching nearly to a third-floor balcony that clung darkly to the side of the mansion.

Cubby stared a moment at the balcony and the tree. Then his eyes moved on, but suddenly they darted back. It was too dark to make out details, yet he was certain something had moved there, within its shadowy branches.

Must have been only his imagination, he decided after peering hard and long. The only thing moving tonight was the faint, chill breeze . . . and not a ghost in sight.

Chapter Ten

After only about twenty minutes when absolutely nothing happened, Cubby got bored waiting for Andy's ghosts to appear. "There ain't no ghost going to show up tonight," he said quietly, trying not to let Andy hear the chattering of his teeth.

"She don't come out every night," Andy came back.

"I don't think there is any ghost."

"I seen it," Andy retorted, his voice low but firm.

"I'll bet Nan-ta-kee would know about such things as Indian ghosts," Cubby allowed.

"That's all a big story," Andy scoffed. "War Hatchet. Hah! You don't got no Indian name, and I'll bet you never scalped a man in your life, neither. Bet you don't even know no Apache."

"I do too know an Apache."

"Right. And my uncle was General Custer."

Cubby glared at him. "All right, you can make

light of it. But I'm telling you the truth." He hesitated. "Well, maybe except for me scalping anyone."

"Told you so."

"It was Nan-ta-kee what done the scalping."

"Bah!"

"What was that?" Cubby's head shot around and he stared at the dark yard.

"What?"

"I heard a sound. Like something gave out a groan."

"A groan?" Andy looked and suddenly went stiff as an iceberg. Cubby saw it too. A gauzy figure had floated from the side of the house and hovered in the backyard. Paralyzed for the moment, all he could do was stare, his jaw slack, eyes big as double eagles. Neither boy spoke right away.

The apparition floated across the yard, first this way, then that, as if uncertain where it was or where it wanted to go. It paused at one point, then moved toward the toolshed.

Slowly Cubby was regaining his composure, and with it came a more critical eye, something that Andy seemed incapable of managing at the moment. Cubby began to breathe again, his fright draining away, curiosity taking its place.

"S—see, I told you so," Andy croaked.

Cubby leaned slightly forward, eyelids coming together suspiciously as he watched the shed's door creak open on stiff hinges. Suddenly he knew where the groan had come from, and he knew something else too.

"That ain't no ghost, Andy."

The boy's view was transfixed. "Is too."

"That's my Aunt Doreen!"

She'd gotten the door open and was holding a shovel. The night wind caught the silky cloth of her dressing gown and trailed the light material behind her as she stalked about the yard. Cubby could see how it might fool some people into believing a ghost was rising up from the ground. He glanced at the boy sitting next to him, still staring.

"What need would a ghost have for a shovel?" Cubby whispered close to his ear.

"She's gonna dig up her grave," Andy shivered.

Doreen Taylor had selected a spot on the ground and was levering the shovel through the sod and turning it over.

"So, that's what done it." Cubby said. It hadn't been gophers after all. No wonder Charles had been surprised by his question. And by his answer, it could only mean that—Just then that low ghostly groan sounded again and old Charles came into view. Soundlessly he took the shovel from Doreen and worked at the hole.

Andy was coming around just then. "It ain't a ghost." There was disappointment in his voice.

"Told you so."

"What are they doing?"

"Don't know." Cubby and Andy watched the hole deepen. Doreen and Charles worked at it most of half an hour before stopping. Then shaking their heads, Charles refilled the hole, arranged the sod in place, gave it a stomp or two to set it and returned the shovel to the shed. Neither Doreen nor Charles had spoken a word the whole time, and still shaking their heads, they went back to the house. There was that groan again, followed by the soft click of a lock, and that was it.

Andy and Cubby stared at each other, then at the newly dug spot. Nothing had been accomplished as far as either of them could tell.

"That's weird," Andy allowed finally.

It was the first thing the red-faced boy had said so far that Cubby could agree with.

They weren't the only ones who thought Doreen Taylor stealing about her backyard, in her dressing gown in the middle of the night and digging holes, was weird. Six other pairs of eyes had watched the event too.

Hidden among the deep shadows of cottonwood trees, Burl Rahn removed his hat and scratched his itchy scalp. There wasn't much hair left there. A few strands clung to the sweatband of his Stetson. He wiped them out and settled the hat back in place. "Maybe she went an' buried something?" he wondered.

"Didn't see them bury anything, Burl," Langston whispered, moving a bit to his left for a better view of the two people returning to the house. He and Rahn had been in the Bitter-Sweet Saloon when Brawley had come rushing in to tell them that the kid had finally showed. But by the time they all got back to where Brawley had been standing his turn at watch, the boy was safely ensconced upon the porch roof next door, and there was that other boy with him too. They were just trying to figure out the best way to get to him when Doreen Taylor and her black servant had appeared.

"Looks like they are leaving," Rahn said, watching the two boys creep across the roof.

"They're gonna shinny down that tree," Brawley said.

"Here's our chance, boys," Rahn said. "You two grab that chubby kid and make sure he don't see nothing or make any noise. I'll deal with the other."

"What are we supposed to do with him?" Langston asked.

"I don't know. Think of something. Tie him up. Knock him out. Break his neck. I don't care. Just deal with him."

Langston and Brawley exchanged looks. Neither man was happy about what they were about to do, but kept it to themselves.

They left the shadows and crossed to the fence. Instead of the fancy wrought-iron affair that surrounded Doreen Taylor's place, the neighbor's yard was circled by a simple, low picket. The men hunkered alongside it, and looked along the row of dark houses. All was quiet. By the porch, Cubby and Andy had already swung into the low branches and started down.

"Remember, be quick, be silent and we'll be done with it and on our way in a minute," Rahn whispered.

"Let's get this over with," Brawley said.

"Come on." Rahn stood and swung a leg over the fence. No sooner had his foot touched ground on the other side than a flash of black and white streaked out of the shadow, yapping to wake the dead. It latched onto Rahn's leg, sinking teeth into his calf and shaking it like a rat.

Rahn stifled a yell and leaped back out of the yard, leaving the dog there charging up and down the fence trying to get at them.

They dove for the cover of the trees and lit out of there along the stream like all of the Seventh Cavalry was on their tail, and they didn't stop running until they were safely in town and circled around a table at the Bitter-Sweet Saloon.

"That does it," Brawley said, breathing hard and keeping a worried eye bent toward the doors. "I'm outta here in the morning."

Rahn was examining the dog bite, pressing a dirty

116

bandanna to stem the flow from the two deep punctures there. "We're gonna finish it before anyone leaves," he growled. "Tomorrow. We'll get the kid tomorrow."

"Yeah? What about that dog, huh?" Langston demanded. "What about that other kid? We hadn't counted on that." The saloon was practically empty, but one or two heads lifted at the anger in his voice.

"Keep it down," Rahn shot back, glancing around the dimly lit place. "We can handle one little mongrel dog. And as for the friend, I'll take care of him too if he's there."

Brawley frowned.

Langston said, "What if the kid doesn't show tomorrow night? Huh? Then what?"

"Didn't Brawley say that he came out of a window and down the fire escape? If he doesn't show, I'll just slip into his bedroom and do the job while he's asleep. But one way or another, we ain't leaving until the job is done."

Brawley said, "Sounds to me like you got this stuck in your craw, Burl."

"It's become personal," Rahn shot back.

"For you, maybe, but not for me, and not for Kleef either."

"One more day, that's all. If it don't pan out, then we'll pull out. But mark my words, if we don't finish off that kid here and now, you, me, we are always gonna be looking over our shoulders for the rest of our days, wondering if that knock on the door ain't the law. He ain't gonna forget our faces, but ten years from now when he's all grown up, we won't know his. Do you want to live out the rest of your lives never knowing when the law is gonna catch up with us?" Rahn gave a snort when he read the looks on their faces. "I didn't think so."

He'd put down the mutiny, but this was the last time, and Rahn knew it. If they couldn't get the kid tomorrow, Brawley and Langston were heading home.

When Huck began his barking, Andy and Cubby were inside the branches of the little elm and couldn't see what the problem was. As soon as Andy lighted upon the ground, he called the dog and gave him a good scolding for making such a racket. Wagging its tail, the pup romped happily about their heels.

"I better be getting back inside, in case Aunt Doreen comes looking to see if I'm still asleep." Cubby started over the fence into his yard.

"Hey, see you tomorrow?"

Cubby looked back and in the darkness saw the eagerness burning in Andy's face. This was the sort of adventure that lit his imagination. "Yeah, sure, I'll see you tomorrow."

"We can make plans for tomorrow night, okay?"

"Okay."

Cubby climbed the fence, slipped past the withered garden and up the stairs, folding himself through the window. As he crawled out of his clothes and washed his face and hands in the now cold water, he wondered about what he had seen tonight. It had made no sense to him, but then that didn't mean much. There was much grown-ups did that made no sense to him. Still, this was so very much different from what he was used to that he had to wonder what his Aunt Doreen was up to and if maybe she was fishing with a tangled line. He thought maybe he ought to tell Nantaje, or the major, or maybe it was Captain Louvel who ought to be told? He just didn't know what to think, as he crawled under the blankets and pulled them to his chin.

He glanced at the window still opened a crack and letting the chill night air spill in. He thought he should shut it, but before he could pull himself from bed, his eyes closed and he was fast asleep.

If Cubby and Andy were confused by the night's events, two of the watchers there were not. Stationed nearby in the shadows, they had witnessed everything, and unlike Cubby, they knew exactly what Doreen Taylor was doing. But they weren't talking to anyone about it. What they didn't understand, however, was what those three who had been attacked by the dog had been up to.

They'd have to keep an eye on them, they decided. If Doreen Taylor's pattern kept true, she only hunted a little while each night, and then went off to bed.

Their work was through for the night.

Moving out of their hiding place, the shorter of the two commented, "One of these days."

"Patience," the taller one noted, nodding his head.

"William ought to be told about those three—and the ones that came into town this morning."

"We'll wire him tonight," the taller one said as they strolled off down the dark street.

They had seen everything—or so they thought. But they had completely missed the sixth pair of eyes. Those *had* seen everything, and now as they watched the two men receding down the street, a shadowy form dropped silently down out of the huge elm at the corner of the house and with the stealth of a hunting cat, swiftly followed at their heels.

Chapter Eleven

Morning was but a faint glow upon the windowpane when Keane turned heavily upon the bed and looked across the tiny room. He frowned. Louvel's bed had not been slept in, the covers still neatly in place. Keane swung his feet to the floor and stood, leaning upon the windowsill. The street beyond was practically deserted this early. A dog darted across it while a milk van made its way toward the Rimrock Café. The driver pulled up there, hopped off the seat and went around back of the wagon and hauled a basket of bottles into the café.

Keane dressed, splashed water onto his face, and buckling on his gun belt, pulled open the door and started down the narrow hallway. A door opened and Nantaje slipped quietly out, pulling it gently closed behind him. Keane stopped. His view took in the three doors of the rooms he had rented. "O'Brian and Ridere in there still?" he asked, nodding at one of the doors.

"You cannot hear O'Brian snoring?" the Apache asked.

Keane grinned. He could hear the Irishman gently sawing away, now that the Indian had mentioned it. "How about Lionel?"

"He is still asleep," Nantaje said, glancing briefly at the door he'd just come from.

"Captain Louvel never made it home last night."

Nantaje gave one of his rare smiles. "He and the lady spent the night together?"

"I doubt it. Not Louvel. You know what he thinks of such carrying on." Keane hooked a thumb at the door to Ridere and O'Brian's room. "He's always riding those two for their loose living." Keane winked. "He's got a reputation to think of."

"You worry about him, John Russell?"

"Me worry about a damn rebel?" Then his lips hitched up slightly. "Well, maybe a little."

They went down the stairs and crossed the parlor to the door. Keane said, "I'm still wondering about those two men we tailed yesterday. It's mighty suspicious, that one following Louvel like he did."

"I would not worry about those two, John Russell." They stepped out onto the deserted boardwalk.

"What makes you say that?"

"I know who they are."

Keane slanted an eye at the Apache. "Your walk last night? I didn't think you just wanted to be alone."

"They work for the railroad."

"Interesting." That was unexpected, but thinking it over, Keane wondered why it should have been.

121

Doreen Taylor had close connection with the railroad before Horace Taylor died.

"They are camped in a railroad car hidden among many others on a siding."

Nantaje and Keane stepped to one side as the hotel clerk emerged with a broom and began sweeping the boardwalk.

"What else did you find out?" Keane asked when they had moved out of earshot.

"Only that they have a telegraph in the car where they live."

"How do you know that?"

"There was a gap in the curtain." Nantaje smiled thinly.

"I'd like to see this railroad car."

"I will take you there."

Keane nudged the Indian and pointed across the street at a horse tied in front of the Iron Rail Saloon. "Isn't that Louvel's?"

"He spent the night in a saloon?" Nantaje wondered.

"Come on." Keane angled across the rutted road. Louvel's horse looked over at them. The southerner's gray uniform blouse was neatly rolled and tied in a bundle on the saddle.

The front doors of the saloon were closed but the handle turned and they went inside. The place was quiet, except for the ragged breathing and occasional snorts from four sleeping men. Louvel was one of them, his head propped upon a pillow on the table, a blanket pulled up over his shoulders. Curiously, each man there had a pillow and blanket. Some had pushed tables together and others just sprawled out on the floor.

An iron accordion barricade was stretched in front of the bar and padlocked, guarding the bottles of liquor. The proprietor was nowhere around. "Looks like this is where the local drunks call home," Keane said.

"It is good someone gives them a lodge to sleep it off."

They crossed the swept floor. "Royden," Keane said quietly and touched his shoulder.

Louvel stirred, then came suddenly awake. He lifted his head from the pillow, straightened up in the chair and smacked his dry lips as he looked around, getting his bearings. Then he remembered where he was and the moment of confusion left his face.

"Major Keane?" he said, stretching. "What are you doing here?" The odor of last night's whiskey was still heavy upon his breath.

"Spied your horse out front."

"Ah should have taken him to the livery."

"I can do that for you," Nantaje offered.

Louvel nodded. "Thank you." He looked around the barroom again. "Ah must have fallen asleep." Then he grinned. "It is not the first time."

Keane and Nantaje pulled around chairs. "Are you all right?" Keane asked.

Louvel pulled himself taller in his chair. "Ah am fine. Ah came here for a drink and a friendly game of cards, and found both." There was irritation in his voice.

"Well, how did it go" Keane asked.

"Go?"

"You know. Dinner with Mrs. Taylor."

"It was wonderful, suh. It was as if Ah had stepped back in time twenty years. We talked of home, of the South."

Keane frowned. "You spent the evening with a

woman you once loved and talked about the past? What about the future?"

Louvel squirmed uncomfortably. "It is much too early to speak of that, suh."

"Yes, yes, I know, but you must have some feelings about it. Like you said, it's been over twenty years, and people change."

"Certainly a lot of time has passed. There is so much catching up that one evening could not possibly do."

Something was wrong, but Louvel was a tight-mouthed man, and Keane was not going to pry. "Why don't you go to the room and wash up while Nantaje and I take your horse to the livery. Afterward, some breakfast will help settle your stomach."

"Ah'm fine."

Keane didn't argue the point. It was plain Louvel was hung over, but it was his doing and his problem. And if he wanted to deny it, that would be of his choosing as well. The harder you pushed Louvel, the tighter his mouth became. Keane had learned that much about the man over the last several months since they met up in Tombstone and had begun riding together.

"Do white men get drunk when they court women?" Nantaje asked later as they made their way to the livery with Louvel's horse.

"It is not a common practice as far as I know."

"Then there is something troubling him?"

"I'd say that was a safe guess."

After putting the horse up, Nantaje showed the way through the maze of railroad cars sitting on the sidings beyond the huge freight buildings. A passenger car, looking out of place nestled in among the ore, cattle, flatbed and freight cars, caught Keane's eye as he and Nantaje slipped out of sight behind a freighter.

"There, John Russell."

Curtains were drawn across the windows, and tendrils of gray smoke streamed from a chimney. As Keane studied it, a door opened and the man he recognized stepped out the back door and stood upon the platform, sipping a cup of coffee. It was the one from the street corner by Doreen Taylor's house. He was a strapping man, wearing the same pants, but he had left his jacket inside the car and stood there in shirtsleeves and vest only. He wore a shoulder holster beneath his left arm, and the nickel-plated revolver caught the sunlight as the man turned toward them. Keane and Nantaje backed out of sight.

"I've seen his kind before," Keane said.

"Why do they watch the Taylor lodge?" Nantaje wondered.

Keane shook his head. He was wondering what it was about Louvel that had caught their interest as well. "Something going on there, that's for sure."

"Maybe we should look into it, John Russell."

"Maybe."

The man went back inside and a few minutes later he and his partner emerged, jackets hiding the hardware, bowler hats low over their eyes. The taller of the two locked the door behind them and they started off into town.

"They're going after breakfast," Keane noted, slanting an eye at Nantaje. "You still know how to do your trick with locks?"

The Apache grinned. "I didn't spend all those years at Fort Bowie keeping my eyes open and my mouth shut for nothing, John Russell."

Keane gave a short, quiet laugh. "Next time I get

125

back down that way I must have a talk with the sergeant of the stockades and let him know what his soldiers are teaching you guys."

"Teach no more," Nantaje said, frowning. "No more Apache scouts. The fight is over. Geronimo is captured and the white soldiers have moved him and all the rest of his band off the land of our fathers and far away to Florida where he must die."

Keane grimaced. He knew the Apaches' dread of being removed from their land. He looked around the ground and found a bent nail and a short, flat sliver of steel. "Will one of these work?"

Nantaje selected the flat piece of steel. They crossed to the car, up the three steps to the platform. Keane stood in front of Nantaje to hide his work at the keyhole. Shortly there was a soft click. Nantaje opened the door and they slipped quickly inside.

The car had been stripped of its seats and in their places were a couple of chairs, two cots and a desk on which was a green-shaded lamp, a pad of paper, two pencils and a telegrapher's key. A small potbellied stove stood off to one side next to a bucket of coal. The pot that sat upon the stove still held some coffee. Keane spied a couple of rifles in a corner, a pile of newspapers on the floor beside one of the cots, a book by Robert Louis Stevenson with a marker stuck between the pages upon the other.

"Pretty Spartan," he said.

Nantaje picked up the key and examined it curiously, then followed the wires to the place where they disappeared.

"Doesn't tell us much, does it," Keane commented, pulling open drawers. Alongside the desk he discovered a wastebasket, but it only held some greasy brown paper, an old newspaper and a couple of wadded-up slips from the pad on the desk. The papers, it turned out, contained ticktacktoe and hangman games. Keane found that odd, considering the telegraph key there.

"The wires go there," Nantaje said, pointing out the window at the telegraph line running alongside the tracks.

"Why are there no messages then?" Keane wondered, glancing around for a cupboard or closet he might have overlooked. There was a little room off to one side with a closed door, and at the foot of one of the cots was a crate of apples. He started for the closed door, but then his eyes came around suspiciously to the stove. He opened the small hatch and there among the glowing coals were the rectangular ashes of a piece of paper. "That's why."

"The words on it must be important for them to destroy them."

"I wonder. . . ." Keane took the pad and held it at an angle to the light, viewing low along its surface. "There is an impression here," he said returning to the desk and lightly shading the paper with the side of a pencil.

Nantaje grinned. "That is clever, John Russell."

"Something I picked up while working in the adjunct's office when I was but a lowly lieutenant. The army taught you how to pick locks, my friend, and it taught me the fine art of C.Y.A."

"C.Y.A.?"

"Covering Your Ass."

Nantaje gave him a blank look.

"I'll explain it to you sometime." Keane looked back at the paper and read it aloud:

CURIOUS DEVELOPMENT *STOP* KEEP STRANGERS UNDER EYE *STOP* IF PROVE PERSISTENT USE WHATEVER MEANS

NECESSARY TO DETAIN THEM *STOP* KEEP
ME ADVISED *STOP* WILLIAM.

"I wonder what strangers the words mean," Nantaje said.

"I take it to mean us—unless there are other strangers in town that I don't know about."

"There are others, John Russell."

"Something else you discovered on your walk?"

"I should have told you. Those three men who killed Cubby's uncle are in town. I overheard them planning to kill the boy. They think he can identify them. I did not go for a walk last night. I was hiding in a tree by the Taylor lodge. The murderers were there too, but they didn't get to Cubby. And we weren't the only ones. The two men who watch the place—they were there too."

"I wish you had told me this sooner," Keane said impatiently. "We need to pull Cubby from that house right now, then go to the sheriff."

"There was another thing I saw last night that was much strange. The woman, Doreen, she was out late at night digging a hole behind her lodge. The black man was with her. They seemed to be looking for something, but did not find."

Keane recalled the mounds of overturned earth scattered about Doreen's yard. "That is strange, Nantaje." Keane ripped the page from the pad and tossed it in the stove. Then he rearranged everything just as they had found it. "We better get Cubby someplace safe, then go see the sheriff."

Just then the door burst opened and in stepped the two men, revolvers drawn and pointed at Keane and Nantaje.

"You two aren't going anywhere," the shorter one

said as his partner came forward and motioned for them to raise their hands.

"Breakfast, John Russell?" Nantaje asked, reaching for the ceiling.

Keane frowned, his eyes fixed upon the shiny gun in the man's hand. He had miscalculated—miscalculated badly.

Chapter Twelve

Overhead, two bronze rods ran the length of the car. Back when this carriage carried passengers and held rows of seats; the rods were convenient handholds. Then the seats had been unbolted from the floor and removed, but the rods left in place, held to the ceiling by dull bronze fixtures every five or six feet. Practically useless now for anything except draping a towel over, hanging a few clothes from or snapping one end of a pair of handcuffs to.

Keane gave a sharp tug. The steel cuffs and bronze tubes were solid. He could pace only six feet back and forth until the cuff, sliding along the tube, encountered one of the fixing brackets. And that was as far as he could go. Across the car, Nantaje was similarly attached. They exchanged glances, then turned toward the two men depositing their guns, Nantaje's scalping knife and whatever else Keane and Nantaje had had in their pockets upon the desk, handily out of reach.

The taller one looked the knife over, dropped it back onto the desk. He counted through the money, about twelve dollars in silver, and spent a moment studying the flat piece of steel he'd removed from Nantaje's pocket. He tossed it back with the rest of the stuff and said to his partner, "Lucky we come back for your watch, Rollo."

Rollo had removed a gold watch from the pocket of a vest that lay crumpled in the corner of one of the cots, and he slipped it into the pocket of the vest he was wearing. He patted the bulge in his pocket and said, "It was a lucky thing, all right, Butch. But I still want to know how they got in and why."

Butch shifted his dark eyes back to Keane and Nantaje, narrowing them along his crooked nose. "All right, I'll ask you two again. What are you doing here?"

Nantaje remained silent.

Keane said, "We thought you guys might have something worth stealing so we broke in." It was a lie that Keane hoped might convince them to turn them over to the sheriff, who was the one he wanted to see anyway.

Butch sneered and shook his head. "I don't believe you. I seen you two with that Taylor woman. What did she do? Hire you? She know we're watching her place?"

"I don't know what you're talking about."

"Yeah, sure. Hear that, Rollo? These two thugs were trying to rob us."

"In a pig's eye," Rollo scoffed.

"I know how to make toughs like you two squeal," Butch said, taking a blackjack from his coat pocket and lightly slapping it on the open palm of his hand a couple of times.

Keane still had one fist free, and if Butch got any closer he'd make him pay dearly for the pleasure of using that sap. But the man with the broken nose didn't make a move. It was clear he was only laying on a threat for the time being.

"How did you get in here?" Butch asked.

"The door was unlocked."

"I always make sure I lock it."

Keane shrugged and gave a grin. "You must have forgotten this time."

Rollo pulled the watch from his vest and snapped open the lid. "Can't want to waste too much time on these fellows now, Butch."

Butch frowned, exasperated, and shot a glance at Nantaje. "What's wrong with you, don't you talk American?"

Nantaje gave him a blank look.

Butch slapped his hand a couple more times, then shoved the leather blackjack back into his pocket. "We'll be back later. Maybe standing here and thinking about it all day will loosen your tongues," he growled.

They put Keane's and Nantaje's revolvers in one of the desk drawers and casting a final glaring look at them, went outside. The lock clicked over and their footsteps sounded on the platform steps. Leaning far forward from the point where he was stopped against the bracket, Keane was just able to catch a glimpse of them through a slit in the curtains. Then they were gone.

"Got any ideas, John Russell?"

Keane gave a jerk on the handcuff and frowned. "Not a one. These shackles aren't going to budge."

"Neither are the bars," Nantaje said, putting his

weight on them. He eyed the desk that held their belongings. If I could get the pick." He stretched, but the desk was a good ten feet beyond his reach.

Keane tested his bar too. It was solidly anchored to the ceiling. He searched for some tool that might help him, but there was nothing he could get to.

"War Hatchet is in great danger," Nantaje said, giving a futile tug at the cuffs.

"I know," Keane replied with the first twinges of desperation beginning to squeeze at his chest.

It was midmorning when Charles drove Cubby to town in Doreen Taylor's carriage. Cubby had never ridden in a really fine carriage, and was surprised when his finger found a split in the seat cushion.

"A saddle maker can fix it up," Cubby told the black man beside him.

"Miss Taylor got better things to spend her money on," Charles replied. The tone in his voice told Cubby to drop the matter.

They pulled up in front of the general store and Cubby followed the old man inside, curious at the look he'd noticed in Charles's face. It was like a man about to face a challenge, though Cubby wondered what kind of challenge it was to buy him the few necessities of life that had been lost in his Uncle Alroy's wagon.

"One pair of trousers and two shirts," Charles whispered to him as they passed down an aisle of lamps and coal oil, shovels and rakes, toward the back where clothes were shelved.

"I need a jacket too," Cubby said.

"You do not."

"It's getting toward fall and the nights are cold."

Charles relented, seeing the necessity of it. "All right then, one jacket."

Cubby glanced down at the scuffed shoes on his feet. The soles were thin and wouldn't last much longer, but Charles was adamant when he inquired after a pair of sturdy boots.

"You think Miss Doreen is made of money?" he asked.

From the show she put on, Cubby was inclined to believe just that.

Charles said nothing more after that and kept his eyes averted so that Cubby couldn't read the expression on his face. Cubby selected the clothes, but Charles had the final say in what he could buy. He'd carefully scrutinized the tag of each item, putting an expensive pair of wool pants back on the shelf, replacing them with a cheap pair of canvas-duck trousers. "These will last longer," was his only comment.

He agreed to a checked cotton shirt, and a wool coat that had been marked down from $3.95 to $3.00. Mentally, Charles tabulated the damages. He hesitated before going to the counter, and appeared to be mustering his resolve over something. Then he escorted Cubby to the counter.

"Good morning, Mr. Kettleridge," Charles said, flashing a smile at the shop owner. "Miss Doreen's nephew has come to visit for a while," he announced, patting Cubby affectionately upon the head. "We need to outfit him with some new clothes."

"Uh-huh," Kettleridge said, looking stern and unfriendly. "You got cash in your pocket, Charles, or is this another one on account?"

"Why, if you don't mind, I think we'll just put it to the account." Charles smiled widely.

"The account is overdue, and as far as I'm concerned my books are closed to Mrs. Taylor until she settles up." Kettleridge put his hands on the counter and just stood there, not making a move toward the clothes they'd placed atop it.

Charles caught his breath and gave Cubby a quick glance, like grown-ups sometimes do when they forget themselves and let go of a curse in the presence of a child.

Kettleridge eyed Charles unswervingly.

Footsteps sounded behind them. Kettleridge's view flicked up and went past Charles.

"Ah couldn't help but overhear," came the easy southern drawl.

Cubby wheeled about. "Mr. Louvel!"

"Cubby," Louvel said briefly, stepping up to the counter. "How much is Mrs. Taylor's bill?"

"Who are you?" Kettleridge demanded.

"Ah am an old friend, suh. And Ah wish to settle up on the account."

"Err, well, in that case . . ." He cleared his throat, opened a small ledger book, ran a slim finger down a column of numbers, then said, "Forty dollars and twenty-seven cents."

Louvel paid it, along with the bill for the new clothes for Cubby. Outside on the boardwalk, Charles shook his head and said, "I appreciate what you done, Mr. Louvel, but Miss Doreen, she's going be powerful upset to hear of it."

"What has happened, Charles? Is Doreen in tight financial straits?"

Charles shook his gray head some more. "I can't say a word 'bout it. You are going to have to ask her."

Cubby was confused by it all. His aunt was obviously rich. Why didn't she pay her bills? Puzzling over it, he caught sight of the familiar freight wagon parked down the street and looked around for Patty.

She wasn't in sight, but there were three or four men eyeing her wagon in a way that made him wonder what they were up to. From the sound of their laughter, Cubby figured they were already drunk for the day.

He wanted to see Patty again, to tell her about his aunt's strange behavior and hear her explanation. As Louvel and Charles stood there discussing things that he didn't quite understand, Cubby eased away from them and started toward the wagon. One of the men there had taken the big iron skillet Patty had used for dinner the previous night and he waved it at his friends.

"Looks like Fat Patty's in town, boys," he hooted and chucked the pan to the ground, grabbing another off its hook.

"You ought to leave them alone, Daniel," a second man warned. "Patty's liable to twist off your ear if she catches you fooling with her eatin' irons like that."

"Wonder what Patty needs with so many of 'em?" he slurred, staring at the medium-size pan.

Just then Patty stepped out of a shop carrying a paper-wrapped bundle. She stopped all of a sudden, glared, then roared, "Daniel McGuire! You put that pan up or ready yourself to meet your maker!"

"Patty, me dear," McGuire said, bowing, and lifting his grinning face toward her. "Was just admiring your pan here."

Shoulders hunched, Patty barreled toward the man. "I've had trouble with you before, McGuire, and I'm not about to put up with your foolishness again." Patty reached for the pan.

Giggling, McGuire shifted hands. His partners were looking worried. Cubby made his way past a couple of men who had paused to watch the antics. Patty made another stab at the pan. McGuire shoved it just out of her reach and laughed.

"Daniel, I wouldn't push your luck," one of his friends warned.

"Patty and me, we go way back, don't we, sweet pea?"

"I've about had it with you," Patty declared, and tossing down her package, she rounded on the man and shot a fist into his exposed gut. McGuire's eyes popped open, breath exploded from him and he folded in half.

Patty took half a step back and came up with a short, powerful jab to his chin. The crack of her knuckles rang like a bell and McGuire's head snapped back as he reeled into the side of her wagon. Patty charged forward.

McGuire managed to move his face a split second before Patty's fist slammed into the timbers of the wagons. Howling and giving out a barrage of the most descriptive mule skinner language Cubby had ever heard, Patty lassoed the man with an arm about his throat and lifted him off his feet and bulldogged him to the ground, pinning him there like a wrestler.

McGuire squirmed beneath Patty's bulk, trying to protect his face as she began hammering blows that would likely send a buffalo to glory.

Seeing his perilous condition, McGuire's two friends shook themselves from their stupor and leaped upon Patty.

She flung one off as easy as shooing a fly, but the other got an arm about her throat and was holding on as if he'd caught a wild bronc. The other got back into the fight and now Patty was flagging under their weight.

A crowd gathered round to watch the spectacle. Cubby dropped his own package and burst through their ranks. "Get off of her," he cried, and seeing that neither of the men heeded his warning, he seized up the nearest thing at hand and leaped into the fray.

Gong! The skillet clunked one of them soundly on the head. The man tumbled off Patty and sat on the ground, dazed. The other, seeing this new threat, raised an arm just in time. The skillet rang again, likely shattering his elbow. Back and forth Cubby swung, wielding that big skillet like Samson had the jawbone of an ass. Cubby sent those two Philistines running for their lives and when they had gone, Patty stood off the third one.

She looked down at him lying there, arms folded over his head and said, "I warned you, Daniel McGuire, now you skeedaddle before I finish what I started here."

McGuire scrambled to his feet hunching over and, holding his midsection, scampered away after his friends.

"Riffraff," Patty declared, brushing the dust from her hands. Then she looked at Cubby and grinned. "You're the first man what ever come to my aid." There was a gleam of appreciation in her eyes and her grin widened. She stuck out a hand to him. He took it. It was the firmest handshake he'd ever gotten from anyone.

Across the street and out of sight, Burl Rahn, Cooper Brawley and Kleef Langston had witnessed the whole thing. Reflexively, Rahn rubbed his knee. It still hurt, and now that he'd seen it happen all over again, his resolve for vengeance only got firmer.

"That kid is gonna pay," he mumbled.

Brawley flicked the butt of his cigarette away.

"Just remember, Burl, if we don't get the kid tonight, Kleef and me, we're out of here."

"I'll get him," Rahn said confidently.

"We've heard that before," Langston scoffed.

Rahn glared at him. "I'll get the brat and we'll be outta of this place before anyone finds the body."

The shadows shifting slowly about the railroad car were the only clock John Keane had to go by, but they told him that the morning was long past. Nantaje worked at the shackles like a relentless animal, but try as he might, he could not pull a hand free or break a link in the chain that connected the two cuffs.

Keane had stopped trying, and was busy hatching a plan that seemed promising to him.

The door opened and the one named Rollo came in. He shut the door behind him, turned a key in the lock and considered the two of them standing there, handcuffed to those overhead bars.

"Ready to talk yet?" he asked, shedding his jacket and sitting behind the desk.

"Already told you everything there is to tell," Keane replied. "Why don't you just turn us over to the sheriff."

"Got a feeling you'd like that to happen," Rollo said, moving the telegraph key in front of him and throwing a switch. After a moment the telegraph began to chatter. Rollo listened to the noise a while, then not hearing anything of interest, he opened the switch and stretched out on one of the bunks.

"How long are you going to keep us handcuffed here?" Keane asked. "My arm is going to wither and fall off for want of blood."

"Until we find out what we want to know." Rollo

punched a pillow into shape and wedged it under his head.

"Then what?"

"I don't know," Rollo said, clearing his throat and closing his eyes.

Keane said, "I got to take a leak."

"That's your problem."

"It will be your problem if I do it right here on your floor. That'll make living quarters right rank for you and Butch."

Rollo parted an eye and swiveled it toward him. "All right," he relented, swinging his legs off the bed and sitting up. "But I'm warning you . . . any funny business, buster, and I'll drill ya. Don't think I won't." Rollo drew a Smith and Wesson from the shoulder holster, then fished the key from a pocket and tossed it across to Keane, keeping well back from the big man.

Keane unlocked the cuff from his wrist and shook his arm, which had gone numb on him. Rollo waved the revolver at a door to the little room Keane had noticed earlier, keeping him in his sights.

"In there."

Keane stepped past the door and discovered there was nothing more than a hole in the floor serving as the privy. By the odor that wafted up through it, it was plain this railroad car had been here for quite some time.

He left there grinning and said, "Mighty ripe. I'd say it's about time to move this car some."

Rollo's face remained unmoved as the revolver directed him back to where the cuff dangled by its chain.

"Standing there is something of a chore for a man of my years," Keane said easily as they neared the desk. "Mind if I knock a stone out of my boot? It's about to wear a hole in my foot."

"All right, but be quick about it."

Keane moved slowly, showing his empty hands. The man was nervous and the last thing he wanted was to make a quick move and spook him. He sat on the corner of the desk and tugged the boot off, reaching inside it. "Such a tiny thing," he mused, peering at his fingers. He smiled up at Rollo. "Hard to imagine such a speck of gravel could cause a man so much misery." Keane reached back and palmed the sliver of steal that was upon the desk as he stood.

"Hurry it up." Rollo flagged the gun impatiently at Keane.

John Keane pushed his foot into the boot, stomped it on the floor, then straightened. "Feels a lot better. Thanks." He returned and clicked the cuff back around his wrist.

Rollo glanced at Nantaje. "How about you?"

Nantaje remained silent, his dark eyes fixed on the white man.

"Doesn't he speak English?"

"Nary a word of it, I'm afraid. He's Apache." Keane repeated the question in the Apache language.

Nantaje shook his head.

"He's got a bladder like a stock tank," Keane told Rollo. Rollo grunted. "Just so long as he don't pee on the floor." He shoved the gun into its holster and went back to his nap.

Chapter Thirteen

Butch returned a few hours later and asked how it was going, giving a glance at their two prisoners, and Rollo said no trouble.

"Have you informed William?" Butch asked, shucking his jacket and grabbing an apple from the crate.

"Not yet." Rollo slid behind the desk and switched on the key. It instantly began to chatter. He listened until it stopped, then tapped it some meaningful way that was lost on Keane. Butch scribbled something on the pad and Rollo looked it over and began tapping away. When he finished he opened the switch and leaned back, looking at his partner. "We'll have a reply in a couple hours."

Butch tossed the apple core out the door, then stretched out on his cot and picked up the book. Rollo slipped into his jacket, adjusted the bowler hat and flipped him the key to the handcuffs. "I'll be back about seven."

"All right," Butch mumbled.

"How about a drink of water?" Keane asked once Rollo had left.

Butch kept on reading.

"How long you going to keep us here?"

The man still ignored him.

Keane frowned. Nantaje gave him a worried glance. The afternoon was mostly spent and Keane knew the Apache was thinking of Cubby, and of the men who had murdered his uncle and were fixing to do the same to the boy.

Keane reined back his growing impatience. So long as one of them was still here, he could do nothing.

"Ah have not see either of them since morning," Louvel said.

Dougal O'Brian scrunched his mouth worriedly behind the tangled beard and scratched at the scar that had been branded into his cheek nearly forty years earlier. "Maybe you and me, we better go through this town and look for them, Harry," he said to Harrison Ridere.

"They'll show up, Dougal," Ridere said easily, yawning.

They were crowded into Louvel's tight hotel room. The southerner was leaning into a mirror and scrubbing a hand across his cheek. "Perhaps Ah should consider another shave?" he wondered aloud.

O'Brian rolled his eyes. "I reckon I need to teach you a thing or two about women."

Louvel looked over, mild amazement in his dark eyes. "You teaching me? Hah!"

Laugh if you want to, but the truth of the matter is, once you begin to change your ways for a woman, you're a lost man. Ain't that right, Harry?" O'Brian gave his friend a nudge.

"Dougal's right," Ridere said.

"You are both wrong." Louvel reached for his hat and shooed them out of the door ahead of him.

O'Brian laughed. "Give that filly a peck on the cheek from me," he hooted.

"Suh, you are insolent." Louvel left them standing in the hallway and made his way outside. The sky was darkening and heavy shadows lay long across the street as he strolled up the main street and turned onto Commerce Street, Doreen Taylor's house looming in the distance. He had anticipated this second meeting all day as a starving man might a feast, but in spite of that, there was something gnawing at him, something vague and undefinable, and just beyond his grasp. It had been there all day, and he had tried to ignore it, but now the feeling was oddly stronger.

Doreen Taylor was lovely in bright yellow taffeta. She greeted him in the grand living room, grasping his hand in both of hers. Charles immediately took his leave and Doreen led him to the sofa, patting the cushion beside her.

"Would you care for a drink, Royden?"

"No, thank you. Not right now, Doreen."

She smiled suddenly. "I sent Christine into town today to buy a goose."

He sniffed the air. "Is that what that wonderful odor is?" he asked, and it took him back again to those earlier days. He'd not had roasted goose since before the war. He'd had little in the way of luxuries all these years. Then he felt the weight return and he asked, "But isn't that extravagant?"

"Nothing is too extravagant for you, Royden," she replied lightly, but he saw through her facade.

"Doreen," he said, taking her hand. "You don't have to do this for me, if money is tight right now."

Doreen looked shocked and Louvel knew he had overstepped his bounds. "What ever makes you think that?"

Louvel grimaced, and told her about the incident at the general store that morning. "You mean Charles didn't tell you?"

Doreen withdrew her hand and said stiffly, "No, he didn't. Charles tries so hard to protect me from these—these unpleasantries."

"What happened?"

"It's not what you're thinking, Royder," she went on quickly. "My husband Horace—was quite wealthy, but I'm afraid he invested much of the money poorly. I do have considerable assets, you understand," she added, her voice firming up, her eyes widening and peering into his. "It is just that the funds are . . . are not accessible to me right now. But I've been working on the problem and shortly I expect to be fully . . ." She groped for a word. "Fully funded."

Louvel was shocked to hear of her plight. "Ah didn't know, Doreen. Ah am sorry."

"How could you know? It's not something I wish to be known."

"But what of Cubby?" he asked suddenly, wondering if the added burden might be more than Doreen could afford, considering her present dilemma.

Doreen's countenance drooped, and for the first time, Louvel noticed the deep lines that cut into the corners of her eyes, and her flaccid cheeks. He blinked, and for an instant he was able to recall Doreen's beauty at sixteen years old. He tried to grasp on to that memory, but lost it again.

"I know it is a bitter thing, Royden, but I am forced to consider an orphanage." She sighed deeply. "If there was only some other way . . ." Doreen touched the corner of her eye with a handkerchief. "There is one in Cheyenne, a good home from what I hear. I've instructed Christine to write the headmaster. Arrangements are already being made," she said, her voice heavy with regret.

"An orphanage," Louvel murmured, shaking his head.

"Don't look so sad, darling," she chirped, her spirits suddenly rising. "It will be the best thing for the poor child."

"Is there no other course?"

"None. It's all settled."

"But once you have your finances in order and you've returned your capital, then—"

"Then we can leave this dreadful place. We can go back to New Orleans, Royden." A thrill filled her voice and her eyes beamed as she clutched his hand and held it tight. "We can build a grand house overlooking the river and decorate it with the finest tapestries and furniture. We can have our portrait painted and hang it in the ballroom. There will be parties again, and all our friends will come and visit us. You will have your office and gentleman's parlor, Royden, and Charles can serve drinks to the gentlemen who come to visit while I entertain the ladies. We'll have servants, and carriages and land, with acres of cane in the fields!"

Doreen stood suddenly and whirled around, her skirts swishing upon the carpet. She clasped her hands on her chest and said, "It will be wonderful—you and me together finally, and things just like they used to be."

Louvel frowned, the uneasiness he'd felt all day a sudden tidal wave that rocked him. Doreen's eyes were wide and glazed, gleaming with the enthusiasm of a child on her birthday.

"But, Doreen, we can't go back to that. That life does not exist anymore. And what friends do you speak of? There is no one left."

"Of course there is. There are the Radcliffs and the Randalls, and Wanda Beauregaurd. And don't forget, the Anderson twins—Robert and John. You remember the Andersons?"

Louvel remembered them. He remembered that Robert Anderson had died at Gettysburg, and his younger brother John had fallen defending Vicksburg.

"The Randall place burned to the ground, Doreen. You must know that."

"Oh, yes. I forgot. But by this time it must be rebuilt. Mr. Randall had such splendid fields of cane, if you remember. And over seventy slaves to work it. I'm sure it is rebuilt."

"There are no more slaves," Louvel said quietly, frightened at what he was seeing. He hardly knew what else to say. But there was one question that weighed most upon him, and he was half afraid to hear the answer.

"If your wealth is such as to afford all of that, Doreen, then surely you could find a place for Cubby?"

"Cubby?" she asked, cocking her head as if wondering where she had heard the name before. "Cubby? Oh, the boy, Darby. No, no, no, Royden. Darby will have to go to the orphanage. What ever would we do with a child underfoot? He'd only get in our way, after all."

John Keane was slumped against the wall of the railroad car when the door opened and Rollo entered. He pushed himself straight and shot a glance across the narrow car. Nantaje had come alert too. It was already dark outside. Keane figured the time at some past seven.

"Any word yet?" Rollo asked, shutting the door.

Butch had been asleep. He sat up groggily and said, "I checked about an hour ago. Just the usual chatter. Nothing from William yet."

Rollo closed the switch and listened a while as the key clicked away. At a pause, he broke in, tapped the key a few times, got a response, then tapped some more. "Still no word," he told Butch, opening the switch to silence the machine.

"Well, can't do much about it tonight, anyway," Butch said, giving Keane and Nantaje a look. They'll keep for a while longer."

"Yeah. They'll keep," Rollo said, fishing an apple from the crate. He tossed one to Keane and another to Nantaje. "Getting hungry, I'll wager," he said and laughed.

Keane kept silent and crunched into the apple. He knew what should come next and he didn't want to delay them with talk.

Butch consulted his watch, frowning. "Now the long haul begins. I'll be glad when this job is over with."

"Yeah, you and me both."

"Anything happen this afternoon?"

"No, nothing. Except that one-armed fellow showed up again."

Butch shook his head and looked at his prisoners.

"Sure wish I knew what that dame was up to. These two aren't talking."

"They will," Rollo said confidently. "Another day of standing there with their arms stuck up in the air like that will serve to grease their jaws. Anyway, we'll have heard back from William by then."

"We better." Butch shrugged into his jacket. "Well, let's get to work," he said, resigned to the long hours that still faced them that night.

When they left Nantaje said, "Figured out yet who they are, John Russell?"

"Not exactly, but I've seen their type before, and I've got my suspicions."

Nantaje jerked the cuff clamped round the overhead bar. "Got to get out of here. War Hatchet will need me."

Keane reached into his pocket and took out the flat piece of steel Nantaje had used to pick the door lock. "Think this might help?"

"John Russell, where did you—" The Apache started to say in surprise, then glanced at the desk where Butch and Rollo had piled their belongings. He grinned, remembering . . . and understanding.

Keane handed it across to him. "You go to the house while I find the sheriff."

What ever would we do with a child underfoot? He'd only get in our way, after all.

Her words stung like acid, and from his place high above them on the top tread of the staircase, Cubby wiped the tears from his eyes, stood and returned to his room, shutting the door behind him. He had had moments of doubt ever since his first attempt to run away, but now he was determined to see it through. He'd be "underfoot" to no one! Cubby knelt by the chest at the foot of the bed, lifted its heavy lid and took out the blanket he'd discovered earlier after some nosing around. He rolled it tight and tied it with a piece of string taken from the kitchen. Slipping on the new jacket, Cubby looked around the dark room one last time and went to the window.

A shape suddenly appeared there and he leaped back, startled. Andy was nearly as startled as Cubby, but he grinned and rapped quickly upon the window glass.

"What are you doing?" Andy asked once inside. He was staring at the bundle slung over Cubby's shoulder.

"I'm running away."

"Really?" In the darkness, Andy's eyes widened with anticipation.

"Really."

"Can I run away with you?"

"You don't want to come with me," Cubby said. "You got a ma and pa, and a house of your own."

Andy seemed disappointed at his good fortune. "Maybe I can just go with you a little way, huh?"

"Well, okay, but only as far as the rail yard. Then I've gotta hop a train and go back to Denver."

"You are so lucky."

Cubby wondered why, if he was so lucky, he wanted so badly to cry. They folded themselves through the window and stood outside in the dark on the fire escape. "Wish I could say good-bye to Nan-ta-kee," he sighed.

Andy chuckled.

"What's that for?"

"You and your imaginary Apache friend. Maybe he's off scalping someone," Andy taunted.

"You can just stay here if you keep that up."

Andy didn't want to be left behind so he promised not to mention it again. They crept down the fire escape, the great iron structure swaying slightly beneath their weight. Cubby refused to look down, his fist squeezing the handrail the whole way, and when his feet were finally on solid ground he let go of it with a long breath. They scrambled over the fence into Andy's yard and hunkered in the shadow of a lilac bush to pet Huck, who had been waiting on the other side, his tail wagging his rear end.

"I'll be back in a little while," Andy assured the dog as he and Cubby started for the low picket at the back of his yard. Cubby tossed his blanket over, then climbed it with the help of a nearby tree limb.

Andy dropped to the ground beside him and whispered, "The rail yard is this way."

They moved toward the cottonwood trees along the creek. As they moved, Cubby caught a glimpse of a camp fire through the trees. He imagined he smelled food cooking and wanted to turn aside and spend some time with Patty again. But he knew if he did, he'd end up going back to Aunt Doreen's house, and he was determined not to do that.

"Bye, Patty," he whispered so that Andy wouldn't hear and turned his eyes toward the dark stand of trees looming nearer. Just then three dark forms separated from the shadows. Cubby saw them first and stopped.

"Andy!" he warned, somehow knowing these men meant trouble.

"Get that one!" a voice barked out of the night. Cubby recognized it at once. How could he ever forget? It belonged to the one responsible for his Uncle Alroy's murder. The one called Burl. And that meant the other two must be . . .

Just then the men plunged from the shadows. Two went for Andy as the leader rushed at Cubby.

Cubby wheeled around and raced back toward his Aunt Doreen's dark house.

Andy gave out with a blood-curdling cry. It was cut off almost at once. Through his fright and the pounding blood in his ears, Cubby heard footsteps crashing through the weeds behind him. They were nearby now and coming on fast. Cubby dropped the blanket that was just getting in the way and put on an extra burst of speed.

Something grabbed at his jacket sleeve.

He darted left to evade Burl's grasp. He was nearly to his aunt's wrought-iron fence. And he might have made it too, but just then his foot caught something unseen in the weeds.

Cubby tried to catch himself, then pitched headlong to the ground. . . .

Chapter Fourteen

Taking that fall turned out to be a blessing instead of a curse. In that instant, Burl Rahn overshot Cubby and by the time he'd hauled himself to a stop and had come around, Cubby's fist had curled about the half-hidden tree limb that had tripped him up. Acting more out of instinct than conscious thought, Cubby swung out from where he sat on the ground and smacked Rahn hard in the kneecap—the same knee he'd battered a few days earlier with the frying pan.

Rahn let out with a howl and grabbed his knee and hobbled back against Andy's picket fence and cursed the boy.

Cubby shot to his feet and took off. He made his Aunt's fence in half a dozen strides, leaped for the overhanging branch and scrambled up over it like a monkey.

But Rahn was right behind him. Cubby stole a

glance over his shoulder as the man dropped to the ground inside the yard. His heart pounding like a drum, he turned his attention to the fire escape now looming nearby and his feet slapped the first tread. The stairs clanged beneath him as he strove up toward the landing of the first switchback. Then Rahn's heavy boots rang out on the steps, and the whole contrivance swayed beneath him as the man started up it too.

Cubby dared not look back again. He would have cried out for help if had been able to, if his throat hadn't swollen tight with fear. Drawing on every fiber of strength inside him, he rushed on toward the next landing and the next sharp turn. His room was still far overhead.

Kleef Langston and Cooper Brawley had their hands full with Andy, squirming and thrashing about in their arms. Then Andy bit down on the web of skin between Langston's thumb and finger. Langston yanked his hand away and fanned it, holding back a yelp of pain. The kid gave out with a second terrified scream.

Langston grabbed a fistful of Andy's shirt and shoved it into his mouth, silencing him once again.

"This way," Brawley said, corralling the kicking legs and starting into the trees where the deeper shadows could hide what Brawley knew they had to do. Langston wrapped an arm about the twisting chest and struggled to keep the wad of material in place between those snapping teeth as they rushed the boy out of sight.

"What's going on here?" Patty growled from the darkness. She had heard Andy's screams and had left her cook fire to investigate. "What are you two doing to that boy?"

Her unexpected appearance startled the men. Langston turned toward her and lost grip of the gag. Andy spit it out and cried "Help!"

"It's only a woman! Get her," Brawley ordered. "I'll take care of the kid."

Langston dropped his end of Andy and lunged for the shadowy stranger who had suddenly materialized there. He didn't make two steps before Patty's rock-hard fist shot out and cracked his jaw. A second punch leaped up from down low and drove the wind from him, buckling him over. The third blow spun him around and laid him out cold.

Brawley let go of the kid. Andy crashed to the ground. Brawley's hand grabbed for the revolver at his hip, but before he could get it out Patty whipped out her long-barreled Remington and shoved it into his open mouth. Ramming it in hard, she ran him up against a tree.

"Only a woman?" her gravely voice crackled in his ears as the gun barrel twisted its way deeper.

Brawley gagged and sputtered, his eyes popping. Patty yanked the barrel out, and with a sudden move cracked it against his skull. He went down, out cold.

"Only a woman," she mumbled to herself before turning to check up on the boy.

"You all right?"

Andy struggled to his feet. "Cubby! The other one is after Cubby!"

"Cubby?" Patty's eyes narrowed. "Where is he?"

Andy pointed.

"Come on." Patty tromped out of the trees like a mamma grizzly bear going to do battle and when she stopped to look around, Andy was right at her side. They scanned the dark yard. Patty heard a sudden racket then, and got a glimpse of Cubby fleeing up the stairs. The third man was right behind him.

"We'll never reach him in time!" she cried, starting for the iron fence and wondering how in tarnation she was going to get over that thing. But just then Andy saw something else.

"What's that?"

Patty followed his finger and squinted hard into the shadows. There was movement up high in the big elm tree at the corner of the house. Something like a raccoon was scrambling through the branches, only a lot larger. . . .

"I don't know," she said.

Suddenly a shape emerged from the cover of the leaves and sprang toward the house. It was a man. He caught the third-floor balcony, swung up onto it like a circus acrobat, and dashed along the balcony to its end. Leaping to the top of the railing, he dove across eight feet of empty space to the gutter downpipe, then scrambled up the pipe, onto the roof, and then he was gone.

Patty blinked a couple of times, wondering if she hadn't just imagined the whole thing. But Andy had seen it too. . . .

Patty shook the apparition from her memory and with renewed determination set like concrete in her craggy face, she grabbed onto the iron fence and struggled to get a leg over.

Cubby's legs flew like the wind, the stair treads ringing beneath him as he raced higher and higher up the fire escape, trailed by the sound of Rahn's pounding feet, growing louder. They were right behind him by the time he rounded the last turn. Ahead lay the final dozen steps to the small iron ledge outside his window. But the window was closed, and the room beyond the glass lay dark and unwelcoming.

Cubby topped the last step as Rahn's fingers swiped out and skimmed the back of his jacket. Terrified, he plunged on past the window and slammed into the railing, spinning about with his back pressed to the iron bars. Rahn stopped and just stood there, half bent over and breathing hard.

"You've—you've run your last race, boy," he gasped between breaths, his hand going into his pocket and coming up with something dark. "You've whacked me in the knee for the last time and now I'm gonna finish what Kersten started."

Cubby cast about for a way out of there, but Rahn blocked his only avenue of escape. He glanced up at the roof, too high for him to climb. Looking down made his head swim and he clutched the handrail even tighter.

Rahn took a step forward as something made a soft metallic click and a slender blade leaped from the dark object in the man's hand.

There was only one way out of there now, but it was nearly thirty feet to the ground and fear riveted him to the handrail, fear so great that he couldn't even cry out for help.

Rahn advanced another step.

All at once a blood-chilling yell from overhead shattered the night air and something sprang off the rooftop. Rahn glanced up in time to see the man there diving for him. He threw up his arms, and was slammed to the decking. The two men struggled in the dark, blades flashing in the dim light from a thin moon.

Fear held Cubby against the railing. Rahn managed to roll out from under the other man and leap to his feet. But this newcomer's reflexes were cat quick . . . and then Cubby saw who it was.

Nantaje ducked under Rahn's knife and came up

with his own. The blade found its mark and sunk deep. Rahn staggered back hard against Cubby and the iron railing snapped on one corner and bent outward. Instinctively, Cubby's fists welded themselves to the metal as his feet swung out, and then there was nothing below him.

Rahn tottered on the edge a moment, grabbing for the boy as he went over. Nantaje dove and snatched Cubby about the waist. Rahn's weight pulled them both over the edge but Nantaje grabbed the bars at the last instant and the two of them swayed there three stories up as the solid thud of Rahn hitting the ground reached Cubby's ears.

There was another sound as well, like wood snapping and shattering, but Cubby was too petrified to care at the moment.

"War Hatchet, you must climb up," Nantaje said.

But swinging there so far above the ground paralyzed him. Cubby had never been very good with heights.

"I . . . I can't."

"You must. I can not hold on much longer," Nantaje said through clenched teeth.

Cubby knew what he must do. He reached out, his fingertips brushing the iron landing. He tried again, getting a grip this time, vaguely aware of the drumming of footsteps somewhere below him. Firming up on the iron, he pulled himself up, feeling Nantaje giving him what little help he could. He got a second grip, then a knee, and then he pulled himself to safety.

Turning back, Cubby grabbed Nantaje's wrist and held tight. "Use your other hand!" he cried. The Apache was slipping. Cubby could feel the Indian's fingers opening. Then someone nudged him aside, big shoulders pushing their way past him.

Nantaje's fingers opened, but John Keane had clamped onto his wrist by that time and as if plucking a babe out of a perambulator, the big ex-army major heaved Nantaje to safety.

There was quite a crowd gathered around Horace Taylor's flower garden by the time Keane, Nantaje and Cubby made it back down. Louvel and Doreen had rushed from the house at the sound of the commotion, followed closely by Christine and Charles. Patty was there, with Andy, and Andy's mother and father, having heard the commotion as well. And so was the sheriff, whom Keane had summoned and brought with him.

Rahn had landed square in the center of the old garden, and the impact of the fall had opened a vault hidden beneath it. He lay at the bottom now, a good six feet down. That was somehow appropriate, Keane mused.

Doreen stared, her mouth open. Scattered about beneath the body were bars of gold and sacks of coins. "I've found it!" she declared. "I've finally found it."

"No wonder Mr. Taylor loved that garden so much," Charles said, shaking his gray head.

"What's this all about?" the sheriff demanded, looking down at the twisted body. "Who is that man? And who are you?" He turned to Keane.

"I can explain it, sheriff," Keane said, "but first let's get that fellow out of there."

Nantaje lowered himself into the hole, avoiding the splintered wood that stuck out in all directions and heaved Rahn up to Keane, who lifted him from the hidden vault and laid him to one side. Then Nantaje began passing up the bars and sacks.

"Royden, it's all here," Doreen gushed, forgetting

the crowd gathering around them. She fell to her knees, raking the money into her arms, a hopeless task for one woman—or even five. She shooed everyone back and spread herself over the pile like a chicken gathering her chicks beneath her wings.

"Charles, help me take it into the house," Doreen said quickly. "Royden? Christine?" She glanced up only to discover everyone was staring at her.

"You're not taking that money anywhere," a voice barked, and Butch and Rollo stepped forward.

"And just who are you?" the sheriff asked.

Butch stuck a hand inside his coat and flashed an opened wallet at the sheriff. "Pinkerton agents. I'm Butch Hagerty and this is Rollo Fox."

Rollo moved to take possession of the gold.

"We've been watching this place for months," Butch went on, returning the wallet to his inside pocket. "Knew he had buried it somewhere on the property. The question was, where? It was plain that even his wife didn't know."

Doreen clawed Rollo away from the gold, then covered the loot with her body.

Rollo backed off.

Butch said, "Horace Taylor had been embezzling money from the Union Pacific for years. But it wasn't until after he died and the thievery stopped that the railroad figured out what had happened. They hired our agency to find it."

"Of course. William Pinkerton," Keane said, recalling the name they'd used more than once. "I should have put it together. I knew his father, Allan Pinkerton, during the war."

Butch glanced over, his expression widening at discovering Keane there. "How'd you get free?"

"Ask him." He jabbed a thumb at Nantaje.

Butch eyed the Indian. "But he don't talk."

"I do sometimes," Nantaje said in his best English, which at times could be quite good. He flipped the sliver of steel to him. "Picked the lock with that. Those Hiatt Darby shackles are really very simple."

The sheriff took possession of the gold over the objections of the Pinkerton men. Doreen was gently led inside the house by Charles. Defeated, she kept babbling about the parties she would have and the old friends she would invite. Louvel looked on, his stern face unmoving, but the sadness in his eyes could not be hidden.

The crowd broke up. Some of the men carried Rahn's body away, while a couple of others recovered Brawley and Langston from where Patty said she'd left them. Cubby grabbed Andy by the shirt-sleeve and tugged him over.

"This is my friend, Nan-ta-kee," he said, introducing the boy to him.

Andy just stood there staring. "Gosh," he managed, his eyes huge. Then he swallowed and said, "Are you really an Apache?"

"Why, sure he is," Cubby replied.

"I saw you fight." Nantaje put a hand upon the speechless boy's shoulder. "Another brave warrior. Like you, War Hatchet," he said with a glance at Cubby.

"You really do know an Apache!"

"Sure do," Cubby said, puffed up some.

Two days later they were gathered on the boarding platform at the Union Pacific Depot.

"Train departing in ten minutes," a conductor announced, making his way along the nearly deserted platform.

"Wonder where he is?" O'Brian asked, squinting up the street, into town.

161

Keane wondered too. Louvel had not made up his mind yet what his plans were. Was he staying or was he leaving? All any of them knew was that he had gone back to see Doreen Taylor, promising one way or another to meet them at the depot before the train pulled out.

"He will stay with her," Ridere said confidently.

Neither Nantaje nor Lionel had an opinion.

Keane just didn't know.

Cubby stood near the Indian, clutching a carpetbag that held the few clothes he owned. It had been decided that Cubby would go with them, at least until they could find someone who wanted a boy of their own to raise . . . to love. He'd hoped to say good-bye to Patty before he left, but the mule skinner had pulled out early yesterday morning, leaving him disappointed and feeling vaguely empty inside.

At least Andy was not there to see them off. Andy had not given Nantaje's ear a rest since the two had been introduced.

After she'd lost the gold her husband had embezzled from the railroad, Doreen Taylor had retreated into her huge house, refusing to see anyone except Louvel. The turn of events had plunged Louvel into a dark mood these last couple of days. He'd hardly spoken a dozen words the whole time.

The steam whistle shrilled, reminding those passengers not already boarded that the train would be pulling out soon.

"I'll bet Harry is right," O'Brian said, pinching aside some whiskers that had strayed in front of his mouth. "Bet Louvel ain't even gonna come by and give his adios."

Keane suddenly gave a grin. "Make that bet and you will lose your money, Dougal," he replied, looking past the Irishman's shoulder.

O'Brian turned.

Louvel was trudging up the gravelly roadbed from the rear of the waiting train where the livestock cars were located. The outcasts came together to hear what he had to say—all except Lionel, who remained apart, leaning against the depot wall.

Louvel's poker face, as usual, was unreadable.

"Well, Captain?" Keane asked. "Have you come to see us off?"

Louvel frowned, then shook his head. "No, Ah'm coming with you. Ah've just put my horse aboard the train."

"What happened?" Keane asked, concerned.

He grimaced. "Let's just say that Mrs. Taylor and Ah have taken different paths. Our lives have become very different since those halcyon days before the war."

"In other words, you've each changed?"

Louvel nodded. "Ah left her with some money, and Charles says they will be selling the house."

"That happens," O'Brian said.

Louvel nodded again. "Ah suspect she is suffering from delusions too. As Ah was leaving, she kept talking about old friends we each knew, about our lives as they were twenty-five years ago. She seemed not to realize the times have changed." Louvel glanced up sharply, a twitch at the corner of his mouth. "It has opened my eyes to a few things too," he said thoughtfully, glancing across at Lionel standing there.

"Excuse me, Ah believe there is someone I need to apologize to." Louvel walked across the boarding platform to the black man.

"I've never seen Louvel so down in the mouth like that," Ridere said.

"Yeah, he sure is acting different," O'Brian agreed.

"He is a man who has looked at the reflection of his own face, and does not like what he sees," Nantaje noted.

Keane shook his head. "Sometimes a woman can do that to a man, especially one who has changed so like Mrs. Taylor has."

The train's whistle gave a final warning and the conductor was calling all passengers aboard.

Keane said, "Shall we?" and he waved an arm toward the waiting car. "California is only a few days off." Keane dropped a big hand upon Cubby's shoulder and started him toward the train.

From the street in front of the depot came the rattling of harness chains and the rumble of a heavy wagon rolling to a stop.

"Patty!" Cubby chirped happily.

The woman climbed off the high seat and came over. "I just got word you fellas was leaving," Patty said, shifting the chaw in her cheek.

"We are going to California," Cubby told her.

"So I heared. Went to look for you and that sour-faced maid of your aunt's gave me the boot."

"Sorry," Cubby said.

"Don't bother me none," Patty said with a laugh. "I jest consider the source."

"I'm glad you came to say good-bye," Cubby said.

Patty narrowed an eye at Keane. "What's your plans for this here boy?"

"Figured Cubby could ride with us a while, at least until we can find someone who wants to take him in."

"That what you want, Cubby?" she asked him.

"I . . . I guess so."

Patty stroked her chin thoughtfully, finding a hair

between her fingers and plucking it out. "Tell you the truth, I was sorta thinking maybe you'd want to ride with me," she said.

"Really?" Cubby beamed.

"I could use a man's help with the rig, you see," she went on quickly, hiding the gentle tone that had come to her voice.

"All aboard!" The conductor gave the final warning.

Cubby glanced at Keane.

"It's up to you," the ex-army major said.

"While we're confabulating out here, our train is leaving!" O'Brian said as a gush of steam escaped the engine.

"You don't mind?" Cubby asked.

Keane grinned. "I think Patty will take real good care of you."

Lionel, Louvel, Ridere and O'Brian dashed for the moving car.

"John Russell?" Nantaje said, casting a worried eye at the leaving train.

"I will take real good care of him, Mr. Keane," she said.

Keane nodded. "I have no doubt about that." He put out a hand and gave the boy a man-sized shake. "Take care of yourself."

"Bye, Mr. Keane."

Keane sprinted for the car and leaped through the moving doorway.

Nantaje lingered a moment longer. "War Hatchet. I wish you a good life."

Cubby took his hand, not wanting to let go for some reason. "Thanks, Nan-ta-kee. Thanks for everything." Then the last of the stock cars rolled by. Nantaje gave him a grin and, sprinting along the platform, he leaped to the iron hand rungs of the final car and scrambled up to its top. Standing there and looking back, he gave Cubby a wave.

Cubby and Patty remained on the platform until the train was out of sight, then Patty said, "Got a load of chicken wire bound for Franktown, Cubby. What do you say we get these mules on the road?"

Cubby thought that sounded like a grand thing to do, feeling suddenly safe and happy as Patty's big, rough hand folded around his and took him back to her waiting wagon.

⊕UTCASTS
THE OUTCAST BRIGADE

JASON ELDER

They are not wanted where they come from. They are not welcome anywhere. They are outcasts, rootless and friendless, until luck or destiny throw them together. A former Apache scout shunned by his tribe, an ex-Union Army major, a former Confederate captain, and two army deserters, all forced to band together to stay alive—as long as they can avoid killing each other. Can they bury their anger and work together long enough to do what they have to do? Can they make it to Mexico to rescue a band of friendly Apaches who have been captured and sold into slavery? It is no easy task, because even if they manage not to kill each other, there are plenty of others eager to do it for them.

___4699-7 $3.99 US/$4.99 CAN

Dorchester Publishing Co., Inc.
P.O. Box 6640
Wayne, PA 19087-8640

Please add $1.75 for shipping and handling for the first book and $.50 for each book thereafter. NY, NYC, and PA residents, please add appropriate sales tax. No cash, stamps, or C.O.D.s. All orders shipped within 6 weeks via postal service book rate. Canadian orders require $2.00 extra postage and must be paid in U.S. dollars through a U.S. banking facility.

Name _____
Address_____
City_____ State _____ Zip _____
I have enclosed $ _____ in payment for the checked book(s).
Payment <u>must</u> accompany all orders. ❑ Please send a free catalog.

OUTCASTS

BLACK JUSTICE

JASON ELDER

They are a rootless bunch, friendless and unwanted, shunned by everyone except each other. They are the Outcasts, a ragged group of men who make their own way through an unforgiving West, and who know what it is to be hated. And who recognize injustice when they see it. So when they see an innocent black wrangler framed for a murder he didn't commit, it sticks in their craws. Some of the townspeople call the sham trial "Black Justice." To the Outcasts it's just a legal excuse for a lynching. Either way, an innocent man has an appointment with the hangman—unless the Outcasts can find the real murderer in time.

___4744-6 $3.99 US/$4.99 CAN

Dorchester Publishing Co., Inc.
P.O. Box 6640
Wayne, PA 19087-8640

Please add $1.75 for shipping and handling for the first book and $.50 for each book thereafter. NY, NYC, and PA residents, please add appropriate sales tax. No cash, stamps, or C.O.D.s. All orders shipped within 6 weeks via postal service book rate. Canadian orders require $2.00 extra postage and must be paid in U.S. dollars through a U.S. banking facility.

Name_____

Address_____

City_____State_____Zip_____

I have enclosed $_____ in payment for the checked book(s).

Payment <u>must</u> accompany all orders. ☐ Please send a free catalog.

CHECK OUT OUR WEBSITE! www.dorchesterpub.com

Genevieve of Tombstone

John Duncklee

Tombstone in the 1880's is the toughest town in the West, and it takes a special kind of grit just to survive there. Ask the Earps or the Clantons. But among the gunslingers and lawmen, among the ranchers and rustlers, there is Genevieve, a woman with the spirit, toughness—and heart—the town demands. Whether she is working in a fancy house or running her own cattle ranch, Genevieve will not only survive, she will triumph. She is a woman who will never surrender, never give in—and one that no reader will ever forget.

___4628-8 $4.99 US/$5.99 CAN

NIGHT
OF THE
COMANCHE
MOON
T. T. FLYNN

Ann Carruthers has no idea what searching for her brother in the wild New Mexico Territory will me: But what else can a girl, even an English girl not much pa: *wenty*, do when her brother vanishes? How can she know that bandits, Indians, and violence are things people in the territory live with every day? Ann doesn't realize how much danger she is in until the son of a Comanche chief offers one hundred horses for her. To save herself she has to pretend to belong to John Hardisty. Sure, he is a loner and a hardcase, but he can ride, shoot, and fight. And he is her one chance of survival in the lawless wilderness.

___4689-X $4.50 US/$5.50 CAN

TRAIL OF ROGUES
FRED GROVE

Jesse Wilder is a man haunted by too much killing. It started with the slaughter at Shiloh and continued as the young Tennessean fought for his homeland through the horrors of the War Between the States. But what's waiting for him on the treacherous Butterfield Trail in the wild New Mexico Territory might be the worst yet. The settlers' wagons are being attacked. The army assumes it's the bloody work of Apache raiding parties. But battle-sharpened instincts warn Jesse that it's something just as deadly . . . but far more sinister. Now Jesse has to lend all his skill and courage to the army he once fought as they track down a band of cold-blooded killers on the trail of rogues.

___4685-7 $3.99 US/$4.99 CAN

Dorchester Publishing Co., Inc.
P.O. Box 6640
Wayne, PA 19087-8640

Please add $1.75 for shipping and handling for the first book and $.50 for each book thereafter. NY, NYC, and PA residents, please add appropriate sales tax. No cash, stamps, or C.O.D.s. All orders shipped within 6 weeks via postal service book rate. Canadian orders require $2.00 extra postage and must be paid in U.S. dollars through a U.S. banking facility.

Name_____
Address_____
City_____State_____Zip_____
I have enclosed $_____ in payment for the checked book(s).
Payment <u>must</u> accompany all orders. ❑ Please send a free catalog.

MAN
WITHOUT
MEDICINE
CYNTHIA HASELOFF

Daha-hen's name in Kiowa means Man Without Medicine. Before his people were forced to follow the peace road and live on a reservation, Daha-hen was one of the great Kiowa warriors of the plains, fabled for his talent as a horse thief. But now Daha-hen is fifty-three and lives quietly on the edge of the reservation raising horses. When unscrupulous white men run off his herd, the former horse thief finds himself in pursuit of his own horses and ready to make war against the men who took them. Accompanying him on his quest is Thomas Young Man, a young outcast of the Kiowa people. During the course of their journey, Daha-hen adopts Thomas and teaches him the ways of the Kiowa warrior. But can Daha-hen teach his young student enough to enable them both to survive their trek—and the fatal confrontation that waits at the end of it?

___4581-8 $4.50 US/$5.50 CAN

Dorchester Publishing Co., Inc.
P.O. Box 6640
Wayne, PA 19087-8640

Please add $1.75 for shipping and handling for the first book and $.50 for each book thereafter. NY, NYC, and PA residents, please add appropriate sales tax. No cash, stamps, or C.O.D.s. All orders shipped within 6 weeks via postal service book rate. Canadian orders require $2.00 extra postage and must be paid in U.S. dollars through a U.S. banking facility.

Name_____
Address_____
City_____ State_____ Zip_____
I have enclosed $_____ in payment for the checked book(s).
Payment <u>must</u> accompany all orders. ☐ Please send a free catalog.
    CHECK OUT OUR WEBSITE! www.dorchesterpub.com

NEW HOPE

Ernest Haycox

New Hope combines three of Ernest Haycox's finest short novels with the interconnected stories he wrote about New Hope, a freighting town on the Missouri River in what was then Nebraska Territory. In "The Roaring Hour," Clay Travis, the new town marshal, and his fiancée, Gail, are up against the combined forces of the gambling hall owner, the sheriff controlled by him, and the local outlaw leader. A young upstart holds up a stagecoach in "The Kid from River Red" to prove his manhood and impress an outlaw. "The Hour of Fury" tells the tale of Dane Starr, who has come to town to lose his identity as a gunfighter and instead finds himself at the center of a dangerous power struggle.

___4721-7 $4.50 US/$5.50 CAN

Dorchester Publishing Co., Inc.
P.O. Box 6640
Wayne, PA 19087-8640

Please add $1.75 for shipping and handling for the first book and $.50 for each book thereafter. NY, NYC, and PA residents, please add appropriate sales tax. No cash, stamps, or C.O.D.s. All orders shipped within 6 weeks via postal service book rate. Canadian orders require $2.00 extra postage and must be paid in U.S. dollars through a U.S. banking facility.

Name_____
Address_____
City_____ State _____Zip _____
I have enclosed $ _____ in payment for the checked book(s).
Payment <u>must</u> accompany all orders. ❑ Please send a free catalog.

LEGEND OF A BADMAN
RAY HOGAN

In the title novella of this collection, Ray Hogan uses all of his storytelling powers and his keen eye for character to recreate the life and times of frontiersman Clay Allison. Hogan looks beyond the rowdy reputation and past the gunfights to portray a man of integrity, willing to put his life on the line for what he believes in. Was Allison a western Robin Hood, defending the poor and weak? Was he a vicious killer who gunned down more than twenty men? Or is the truth somewhere in between? In this masterful tale, Ray Hogan presents not the rumors, but the truth—not the myth, but the man.

___4560-5 $4.50 US/$5.50 CAN

Dorchester Publishing Co., Inc.
P.O. Box 6640
Wayne, PA 19087-8640

Please add $1.75 for shipping and handling for the first book and $.50 for each book thereafter. NY, NYC, and PA residents, please add appropriate sales tax. No cash, stamps, or C.O.D.s. All orders shipped within 6 weeks via postal service book rate. Canadian orders require $2.00 extra postage and must be paid in U.S. dollars through a U.S. banking facility.

Name_____
Address_____
City_____State_____Zip_____
I have enclosed $_____ in payment for the checked book(s).
Payment <u>must</u> accompany all orders. ❑ Please send a free catalog.
      CHECK OUT OUR WEBSITE! www.dorchesterpub.com